As Ginger untied ribbons and laughed at silly cards and opened her packages, she was aware that the woman by the window was watching her every move.

Once, Ginger frowned at the woman, hoping she would take the hint. The woman responded with a sad look and kept staring.

As Ginger thanked her family and Karie for their gifts, she felt a hand on her shoulder.

She looked up, into the face of the woman who had watched her all through lunch. Involuntarily, Ginger leaned away from the woman's touch.

"Happy birthday, Ginger," the woman said. She was a small woman, and she spoke softly, directing her words to Ginger, as if no one else were in the room.

A chill of apprehension prickled the hair on Ginger's neck. She knows who I am, Ginger thought, but I don't know her.

"As events unfold, suspense builds. . . . This enjoyable novel will draw readers' interest and keep them turning pages." —*School Library Journal*

Also by Peg Kehret:

Cages
Earthquake Terror
Nightmare Mountain
Searching for Candlestick Park

I'm not who you think I am

PEG KEHRET

PUFFIN BOOKS

For Bob Kehret,
who lives with purpose and
coaches with honor

PUFFIN BOOKS
Published by the Penguin Group
Penguin Putnam Books for Young Readers,
345 Hudson Street, New York, New York 10014, U.S.A.
Penguin Books Ltd, 27 Wrights Lane, London W8 5TZ, England
Penguin Books Australia Ltd, Ringwood, Victoria, Australia
Penguin Books Canada Ltd, 10 Alcorn Avenue, Toronto, Ontario, Canada M4V 3B2
Penguin Books (N.Z.) Ltd, 182-190 Wairau Road, Auckland 10, New Zealand

Penguin Books Ltd., Registered Offices: Harmondsworth, Middlesex, England

First published in the United States of America by Dutton Children's Books,
a division of Penguin Putnam Books for Young Readers, 1999
Published by Puffin Books,
a division of Penguin Putnam Books for Young Readers, 2001

3 5 7 9 10 8 6 4 2

THE LIBRARY OF CONGRESS HAS CATALOGED THE DUTTON EDITION AS FOLLOWS:
Kehret, Peg.
I'm not who you think I am / by Peg Kehret.—1st ed.
p. cm.
Summary: Thirteen-year-old Ginger becomes the target of a disturbed
woman who believes that Ginger is her dead daughter.
ISBN 0-525-46153-1
[1. Stalking—Fiction. 2. Mentally ill—Fiction. 3. Mothers and daughters—Fiction.]
I. Title. PZ7.K2518Iae 1999 [Fic]—dc21 98-33879 CIP AC

Puffin Books ISBN 0-14-131237-8

Printed in the United States of America

I'm not who
you think I am

Chapter One

GINGER FELT SOMEONE STARING at her. She had an uneasy sensation, a sixth sense that she was being watched.

At first Ginger ignored the feeling, since most of the people in the restaurant had looked at her when the waiter brought Ginger's hot-fudge sundae with a lighted candle on top.

"Your attention, please!" he had boomed. "We want to wish a happy thirteenth birthday to Ginger!"

Mom and Dad began singing "Happy Birthday to You," and Ginger's six-year-old brother, Tipper, and her best friend, Karie, joined in enthusiastically. Laura, Ginger's older sister, seemed embarrassed and tried to get them to tone down the volume, but by the time they got to "Happy birthday, dear Gin-ger," Laura was singing along.

The family at the next table sang, too, even though they didn't know Ginger, and everyone applauded when Ginger blew out the candle.

A few minutes later, as Ginger scraped the last spoonful of fudge sauce out of the sundae dish, she sensed that someone was still watching her. Curious, she turned and caught the woman staring intently at her.

The woman, who wore a brown blazer over a cream-colored blouse, seemed about the age of Ginger's parents. She sat alone, holding an open book, but her eyes were not on the printed page. She gazed over the top of the book, directly at Ginger.

When Ginger's eyes met hers, the woman did not look away, nor did she smile or nod. Instead she stared harder, as if she were trying to memorize every freckle on Ginger's face.

Ginger whispered to her mother, "Do you know that woman over there by the window, the one with the book?"

Mrs. Shaw glanced discreetly toward the window and then turned back to Ginger. "I don't think so. Why? Does she look familiar?"

"No, but she keeps watching us. I thought she might be a client of yours." Ginger's mother owned a small business, Celebrations; she planned parties and special events. People were always greeting Mrs. Shaw on the street and talking about how nice their anniversary party had been, or their wedding reception, or the company picnic. Sometimes Ginger thought her mother knew everybody in town by name.

Mrs. Shaw looked again, then shook her head. "I don't think I know her."

"Maybe she's a spy," said Tipper.

"Don't be silly," Laura said. "Why would anyone spy on us?"

"She's probably just looking this way, trying to catch the waiter's attention," Mr. Shaw said.

Ginger said nothing more, but she knew the woman was not trying to summon a waiter. She is staring at me, Ginger thought. And I wish she'd stop.

Mr. Shaw glanced at his watch. "It is exactly twelve-thirty P.M.—the time you were born," he said. "Congratulations, Ginger. You are now a teenager."

"We'll never forget the day you were born," Mrs. Shaw said, and she launched into the familiar story of how Ginger was not expected for another two weeks and how they had a flat tire on the way to the hospital and Ginger almost arrived before Mrs. Shaw made it to the delivery room.

"You were such a small baby," Mr. Shaw said. "I was afraid to hold you."

"Five pounds, twelve ounces," Mrs. Shaw said.

"The only thing I remember," Laura said, "is that I got to stay with Grandma and Grandpa, and when you called them from the hospital, Grandma cried. I thought something terrible had happened, until she hung up and told me I had a baby sister. I was astonished to realize that people sometimes cry when they're happy."

"What do you remember about my birthday?" asked Tipper.

"You were our biggest baby," said Mrs. Shaw. "Almost nine pounds."

"And you are the only one to be born here in Seattle," Mr. Shaw said. "Laura and Ginger were born in Texas."

"I think our birthday girl should open her gifts," Mrs. Shaw said.

"So do I," agreed Ginger. As she untied ribbons and laughed at silly cards and opened her packages, she was aware that the woman by the window was watching her every move.

Once, Ginger frowned at the woman, hoping she would take the hint. The woman responded with a sad look and kept staring.

As Ginger thanked her family and Karie for their gifts, she felt a hand on her shoulder.

She looked up, into the face of the woman who had

watched her all through lunch. Involuntarily, Ginger leaned away from the woman's touch.

"Happy birthday, Ginger," the woman said. She was a small woman, and she spoke softly, directing her words to Ginger, as if no one else were in the room.

A chill of apprehension prickled the hair on Ginger's neck. She knows who I am, Ginger thought, but I don't know her.

"Have we met?" Mr. Shaw asked. "I'm afraid I'm not good at remembering names."

The woman started to speak, hesitated, then turned away and walked quickly out of the restaurant.

"That was odd," Mrs. Shaw said.

"How did she know my name?" Ginger asked.

"She's a private investigator," said Tipper. "Your boyfriend hired her to follow you."

"What boyfriend?" said Karie.

"The waiter announced your name," Laura said, "and we all sang 'Happy birthday, dear Ginger.' It wouldn't be too hard to figure out."

That's right, Ginger thought. Everyone in the restaurant knows my name, not just her.

"Could you have repaired a player piano for her?" Mrs. Shaw asked her husband. "Or bought an old player piano from her?"

"It's possible. I'm not as good as you are at recalling names and faces."

7

"I bet she's a scout for ABC Sports," said Tipper. "They're going to offer Ginger a million dollars to broadcast the next Olympics."

"She's probably just a lonely woman who wished she was included in our celebration," said Mrs. Shaw.

Laura, who had come by herself, left to prepare for a party she was catering later that day. The rest of them lingered while Mr. and Mrs. Shaw had a second cup of coffee. Then they gathered Ginger's gifts, the wrapping paper, and the two containers of leftovers, and walked to the Shaws' van.

Everyone piled in: Ginger and Karie in the far backseat, Tipper in the center seat, and Mr. and Mrs. Shaw in front. As Mrs. Shaw maneuvered the van out of its parking space, Ginger looked out the side window and caught her breath.

The woman stood across the street. She held a pencil, and as Ginger watched, she wrote quickly on a piece of paper, glancing once at the van as she wrote.

Did she wait for us to come out of the restaurant? Ginger wondered. Did she write down our car's license number? But why?

Ginger did not tell the others what she had seen. She didn't want to sound overanxious or to spoil the upbeat mood of her birthday celebration.

And, really, what was there to say? That the odd woman had written something on a piece of paper? She could have been adding an item to her grocery list or jotting down a reminder to herself to pick up the dry cleaning.

It probably had nothing whatever to do with me, Ginger told herself. Still, her uneasy feeling persisted. Twice, she turned and looked at the street behind them, fearing that the odd woman might be following in her car. Once, there was a delivery truck in back of them, and the other time there was a red sportscar driven by a man in a plaid cap.

Karie planned to stay at Ginger's house all night. As they started toward the house with her sleeping bag and overnight case, the sensation of being watched prickled Ginger's scalp, just as it had at the restaurant.

She hung back, looking both ways on her street while her parents and Tipper went inside. She saw nothing out of the ordinary. Mr. Colberg strolled along the sidewalk, with his gray poodle, Fluffy, on a leash. A white car was parked in front of the Lawtons' house; the Lawtons often had guests. Brett Konen jumped rope in her driveway.

"What are you looking at?" Karie asked.

"Nothing. It's just—well, that strange woman at the restaurant made me nervous. I know it sounds goofy, but I was afraid she might follow us."

Karie looked startled. "Why would she do that?"

"I don't know. Something about the way she looked

at me gave me the willies. After we got in the van, I saw her across the street, writing on a piece of paper, and I thought—oh, nothing. It was probably my imagination."

Karie looked all around. "I only see a man and his dog, a girl jumping rope, and a fine example of cumulus clouds."

Karie hoped to be a television weather forecaster someday. She had explained the various kinds of clouds to Ginger, but Ginger didn't remember which was which.

Ginger looked up at the fat, fluffy clouds, drifting like huge kernels of popcorn across the blue sky. Cumulus.

"That woman *did* act odd," Karie said, "but I wouldn't worry about it. There are a lot of strange people who are perfectly harmless. Just forget her. You'll never see her again."

Joyce Enderly could hardly believe her good fortune. After years of searching, the girl showed up right under her nose. At a restaurant, of all places.

The girl had changed a lot since that Saturday in Montana, Joyce thought. Her face was rounder and her hair a darker shade. But all kids change in three years' time.

The girl had changed her name, too, which seemed strange. Three years ago, when she escaped at the freeway rest stop, her name had been Lisa, not Ginger.

Joyce still felt sick when she remembered that day. She and her husband had almost made it to their new life, and then Lisa ran screaming out of the bathroom, and Joyce had driven off in a panic without waiting for Arnie to come out of the men's room and get in the car with her.

She had ditched the rental car and hitchhiked to Seattle, where she and Arnie used to live. She changed her name, rented a room, and got a job.

Later she saw on the TV news that Arnie went to prison for abducting Lisa. Joyce felt sorry for Arnie, but she knew if she had waited for him, both of them would have been arrested.

She was relieved that the girl had not recognized her in the restaurant. Of course, Joyce had lost forty pounds and gotten contact lenses after the Montana incident. And back then, her hair had been blonde.

This time, Joyce thought, I'll be smarter. I'll talk to her and win her confidence. I'll tell her who I am and then she'll *want* to come with me and I won't have to use force like we did last time.

Chapter Two

"PEUW!" GINGER SAID WHEN she and Karie went inside. "What's that awful smell?"

"Burned piano keys," said Laura. She was in the kitchen, filling three dozen miniature cream puffs.

"Do I want to know what happened?" asked Ginger.

"I scrubbed some old keys this morning," Mr. Shaw explained. "Then I warmed the oven and put them in, to dry out the wooden part that the key tops are glued to. I turned the oven off and left the keys in it."

"I didn't know they were there," Laura said, "and I preheated the oven to bake cream puffs for Queen Victoria's party. Some of the plastic key tops melted and dripped on the inside of the oven."

"Other kids come home and smell cookies baking," Ginger said. "I smell burned piano keys."

"I'm glad the keys weren't ivory," Mr. Shaw said. "I can't get the ivory ones anymore." He started out the kitchen door, toward his piano workshop. "Ginger, bring Karie out to the shop after a while and see the piano I'm working on. It's a baby grand, and somebody spilled a platter of spaghetti all over the strings."

"How disgusting," said Laura.

"Not as disgusting as the old pianos that are full of mouse droppings," Ginger said.

"This conversation could only happen at your house," said Karie.

Laura finished the last cream puff. "I washed the carrot greens and saved them for you," she told Ginger, pointing to a pile of carrot tops in the kitchen sink.

"Thanks." Ginger stuffed most of the carrot greens into a plastic bag and put them in the refrigerator.

"Nothing unusual ever happens at my house," Karie said.

"That's because you have a normal family," Ginger said. "Be grateful."

Ginger envied the quiet atmosphere at Karie's house, where the phone seldom rang and customers didn't traipse in and out to discuss candles or look at pictures of corsages and cakes. Between Mrs. Shaw's Celebrations business, Mr. Shaw's Old Time Player Pianos, and Laura's B.A. Catering, the Shaw household was usually in chaos.

The rest of her family thrived on the constant activity, but Ginger often wished she could unplug the phone and bolt the door. She couldn't remember the last time she had watched a ball game on TV without being interrupted.

"It would be more peaceful to live at the airport," Ginger said.

"I like all the commotion," Karie said. "It's interesting."

Ginger carried the rest of the carrot tops down the hall to her bedroom, followed by Karie.

Flopsy, Ginger's pet rabbit, hopped out from under the bed and began chewing on Ginger's shoelaces.

"That is not bunny food," said Ginger. She filled his food bowl with the carrot greens. Flopsy munched.

"Who is Queen Victoria?" Karie asked.

"It's our nickname for Victoria Vaughn, Polly's mother," Ginger said. "We call her that because she thinks she's better than everyone else. She's Laura's best customer, but she's hard to work for."

"I like Polly."

"So do I, but her mother's a real pain. Once when

Laura hired me to help her, I tripped and spilled veggies and dip on the carpet. Queen Victoria had a fit. The party hadn't started yet, and she yelled and called me clumsy and told Laura she wasn't paying for the tray of spilled food."

Ginger petted Flopsy as she talked. "While I was cleaning up the mess," she continued, "the first guests arrived, and Mrs. Vaughn miraculously became this kind, forgiving person who explained that she hires local students because she wants to encourage them to work but, of course, young people sometimes make mistakes. She actually had the nerve to smile at me and say, 'No harm done, my dear.' "

"What a two-face," Karie said.

"There I was, crawling around on my hands and knees, picking up broccoli and cauliflower while she put on her good citizen act. I wanted to bite her in the ankle."

"Did she pay for the spilled tray?"

"No. She didn't give Laura a tip that night, either. I couldn't let Laura pay me the ten dollars we had agreed on when it was my fault that she didn't get all her money, so I got humiliated for nothing."

"Why doesn't Laura say she's busy when Mrs. Vaughn calls?"

"Most of Laura's catering business comes from people she meets at the Vaughns'."

"Ginger!" Laura called from the kitchen. "Can you and Karie help me load the van? I'm running late."

They carried out the platter of cream puffs, plates of fresh fruit, and trays of veggies and dip. "She tells people that B.A. Catering stands for Beautiful Appetizers," Ginger told Karie as they worked, "but it really means Broccoli Always."

"Broccoli is healthy, colorful, and easy to prepare," Laura said. "The perfect munchie."

Ginger paused once, fighting back the now-familiar feeling that someone was watching her. A quick glance showed that Mr. Colberg had taken Fluffy home; Brett was now riding her bike; the Lawtons still had company. Tipper and his friend, Marcus, were playing catch in front of Marcus's house. Nothing odd in the neighborhood. No spies. No strangers.

You're getting paranoid, Ginger told herself. One little incident in a restaurant, and you're nervous for life.

After Laura left, Ginger and Karie decided to walk to the park to play tennis. When they told Mrs. Shaw they were leaving, she said, "Would you bring in the mail first, please? I'm expecting a check for a wedding."

As the girls started toward the door, Mrs. Shaw added, "And bring the Lawtons' mail, too."

"Aren't the Lawtons home?" Ginger asked.

"They left yesterday to visit their son in Denver."

Then who is parked in front of their house? Ginger wondered.

The girls walked across the street to the cluster of neighborhood mailboxes.

The car was gone from in front of the Lawtons' house. And so was Ginger's feeling that she was being watched.

Ginger handed the mail to Karie. "Will you take this to Mom for me?" she said. "I'll be right back; I need to ask Tipper something."

She walked to where her brother and Marcus were playing catch. "Did you see the car that was parked in front of the Lawtons' house?" she asked.

"The white one?" Tipper said.

"Yes."

"No. I didn't see it."

Marcus laughed. Tipper looked pleased with himself.

"When it drove away," Ginger said, "did you happen to notice who was driving?"

"It was your boyfriend."

Marcus laughed again. Tipper grinned.

Ginger sighed. "This is important," she said. "Be serious for once."

"He was cute," Tipper said, "and he had a sign that said *Ginger, will you marry me?*"

Tipper and Marcus collapsed on the grass in a fit of laughter.

"I don't know why I bother talking to you," Ginger said.

As she went back home, she heard the two boys singsonging, "Ginger's got a boyfriend; Ginger's got a boyfriend."

If I ever do have a boyfriend, Ginger thought, I won't introduce him to my little brother, the stand-up comedian. Forget about the mysterious car, she told herself. It is gone now, so why worry about who was driving it?

Joyce stayed well behind the van. The last thing she wanted was to arouse suspicion and scare the girl off, like the last time.

As she drove, she pretended to talk to the doctors and nurses at the state mental hospital. In her mind she went back ten years, to the first time she had been hospitalized. She could still see their faces clearly.

"You see?" she said. "I was right and you were wrong. I *told* you my baby lived and was adopted by good parents."

Joyce did not understand why all the doctors and

nurses had lied to her. Why would they say her baby had died?

Joyce had never believed them. Not for one minute. After five months of being hospitalized against her will, she had finally pretended to agree with them because she realized it was the only way they were ever going to let her out.

So she had said yes, she knew the little girl she had tried to take out of Wal-Mart when the child got separated from her family was not Joyce's daughter and that it had been wrong to try to take her. And no, she would never again try to take someone else's child. Yes, she understood that her own baby had lived only an hour.

She said it, but she didn't mean it.

After three months of agreeing with everything the medical staff said, they pronounced Joyce cured, and discharged her. The next day, she had begun searching for the girl again.

It had taken seven years to find her, and then the girl had escaped at that freeway rest stop. Now, through an incredible piece of good luck, Joyce had found her again.

Joyce had been hospitalized in different institutions three times in the years since those first doctors had tried to help her, but it was those early faces she remembered best. They were the first to try to trick her by saying her baby had died.

"What do you say now, you know-it-all doctors?" Joyce muttered.

The van pulled into a long circular driveway in front of a large brick house. Joyce parked on the street and waited. Maybe the girl would come out by herself. If not, Joyce would go in.

Chapter Three

WHEN THEY GOT BACK from playing tennis, Ginger said, "Let's watch the video you gave me."

She opened the video: *Secrets of Successful Sports Broadcasting*. "This looks great," she said.

"Since you're going to be a professional sports announcer someday," Karie said, "I thought you would like it."

"I videotaped the boys' basketball practice yesterday afternoon," Ginger said. "It was my eightieth play-by-play."

"No kidding! You've done eighty pretend broadcasts?"

Ginger nodded. "I've done all the girls' volleyball

games, most of the girls' and boys' basketball games, some baseball games, a couple of swim team matches, and one track meet. Plus a lot of volleyball and basketball practices."

"How can you afford all the blank tapes?" Karie asked.

"I don't save my broadcasts. I erase them and use the tapes over and over. Mom and Dad would never let me buy new tapes for every game or practice. As it is, they think my announcing is a waste of time."

The girls made popcorn, watched the video, and looked at all of Ginger's birthday gifts again.

"I'm starving!" Tipper's voice echoed from the kitchen. "When are we going to eat?"

"Since we had such a big meal this noon," Mrs. Shaw said, "you're on your own tonight. There are plenty of leftovers in the fridge, or fix yourself a sandwich. Laura will be home soon with the extra party food."

"Mrs. Vaughn never keeps the leftovers," Ginger told Karie, "but her guests always eat the best stuff."

Ginger, Karie, and Tipper were making sandwiches when Laura got home.

"Are there any leftover cream puffs?" Tipper asked.

"Nope. Just some stuffed celery sticks and a little fresh pineapple."

"I'll take the pineapple," said Tipper as he added

a pickle to his peanut-butter-and-banana sandwich. "Marcus and I are going to give burping lessons. Do any of you want to sign up?"

"I'll pass," said Ginger.

"It's only ten cents a lesson," Tipper said, "and we can teach you to burp really loud." He took a big gulp of air and demonstrated.

"Guess who came to the party," Laura said as she washed the trays.

"Batman," said Tipper.

"The woman who was at the restaurant," Laura said. "The one who stopped at our table and wished Ginger a happy birthday."

A shiver ran down Ginger's arms and legs. She swallowed hard. "Did you find out her name?"

"No. It was the strangest thing. She arrived in the middle of the party, when it was really busy. I noticed her because she looked out of place. She was wearing that same blazer and slacks, while everybody else wore evening gowns and tuxedos. She came straight over to the table where I was serving, and guess what she said."

"Hand over the cream puffs," said Tipper.

"She said, 'This is the happiest day of my life.' "

"Did she say why?" Karie asked.

"No, and I was too busy to ask her. She hung around for a couple of minutes, and then she said,

'Where is she?' I thought she meant Mrs. Vaughn, so I pointed across the room at her, and for some reason that made the woman angry. She glared at me, took one of my business cards off the table, and left the party."

Ginger picked up her plate. "Let's eat in my room," she said to Karie.

They carried their plates into Ginger's room.

"That woman is giving me the creeps," Ginger said.

"Nothing has really happened," Karie said.

"Doesn't it seem strange to you that, on the same day she stared at me all through lunch, she suddenly appears at a party Laura's catering? She takes a business card but doesn't ask Laura about her rates or available dates. And who did she mean when she said, 'Where is she?' The woman's a weirdo."

"She can't be too much of a weirdo if she was invited to Mrs. Vaughn's house for a party," Karie said.

"Maybe she wasn't invited."

"What do you mean?"

"Laura said she wasn't dressed like the others. Maybe she did follow us when we left the restaurant. She might have driven a couple of cars back, so I didn't notice her. Maybe she parked down the street and watched our house. There was a white car in front of the Lawtons' house, but the Lawtons are out of town. Maybe it was her."

"Someone could have parked there and visited one of your other neighbors."

"It's possible," Ginger admitted, "but not likely. Guests on this block usually park in front of the home they're visiting."

"Maybe it was a salesman, going door to door."

"No salesman came here," Ginger said. She picked up her sandwich, then put it down again without taking a bite. "From where that car was parked, she had a perfect view of our house."

"You sound like Tipper. The woman is a spy."

Ginger wasn't listening. "When our van left again she followed it. That's why the white car was gone when we went out to get the mail."

"Why would she do that?" Karie said.

Ginger was too busy imagining what might have happened to stop and figure out why. "Maybe she waited at the Vaughns' until a lot of people had arrived, and then she went in and talked to Laura. She found out where I live."

"If she followed your van home and parked in front of your neighbor's house," Karie said, "she already knew where you live. Besides, if she was watching you, why would she follow Laura?"

"She saw us loading the van and thought all of us left together." Ginger pictured Laura's business card in her mind. "Now she knows my last name," she said. "And my phone number."

"She probably saw Laura in the restaurant and tried to think why she seemed familiar."

"She stared at me," Ginger said. "When she came to our table, she put her hand on me. She talked to me."

"It was your birthday." Karie began peeling an orange.

Ginger hoped Karie was right; the woman only wanted to hire Laura to do some catering. She hoped it, but deep down, she didn't believe it.

She didn't watch Laura, Ginger thought. She watched me. And she was looking for me at the party.

"I think you're making a tornado out of a rain cloud," Karie said.

Ginger said nothing more about the woman or the white car because she could tell her worries annoyed Karie.

The next day, Sunday, Ginger saw no sign of the woman. No unfamiliar white car parked on the Shaws' street, though Ginger checked several times. She had no feeling of being watched.

Karie was right, Ginger decided. My imagination was doing double-time yesterday, and I scared myself over nothing. She was glad she had not said anything about the white car to the rest of her family.

On Sunday Ginger and Karie hung the poster that Ginger's parents had given her. It said: LIVE WITH PURPOSE AND HONOR.

"When I first saw this," Ginger said, "I thought, yuck, another of my parents' inspirational mottos. But the more I think about this one, the better I like it."

"I like it, too," Karie said. "Especially the first part, 'live with purpose.' Too many kids whine and complain about what's wrong in their lives, but they never do anything to change it."

"Mom and Dad are always telling me to set goals," Ginger said.

That afternoon, the girls experimented with the makeup kit that Laura had given Ginger for her birthday and went for a bike ride. By the time Karie went home, Ginger was relaxed, her fears forgotten.

Joyce Enderly looked again at the business card for B.A. Catering. She longed to dial the number and ask to speak to Ginger, but she wouldn't let herself do it. Not on Sunday, when the whole family would probably be home.

She wouldn't go back and park on their street again

today, either. No, she would figure out how to talk to Ginger alone. Before school, perhaps.

Yes. Tomorrow morning, Joyce would find out which school served the Shaws' neighborhood, and what time classes began and ended.

She would watch and wait until she could talk to Ginger alone. Then later, after Ginger knew the truth, Joyce would get a little apartment somewhere, California maybe, and they would start a new life together. Just the two of them. Just the way Joyce had always wanted.

Chapter Four

AFTER SCHOOL ON MONDAY, Ginger climbed to the top row of the bleachers in the gym to video-tape the girls' basketball game. She was eager to try some of the tips from her new video.

Karie sat beside her. "I promise not to yell into the microphone," Karie said.

"Roosevelt should win this one," Ginger said. "Elk Grove is bottom in the league."

"I'm going to try out again next year," Karie said. "Now that I run every day, I'm a lot faster than I used to be."

"By next fall you'll be so fast Mr. Wren will be begging you to be on the team."

"Not likely. But it was nice of him to suggest that I start running. It's really helped me."

"I would try out myself if I weren't so short." Most of the girls in her grade were two or three inches taller than Ginger, and the ones on the basketball team were the tallest of all. "Too bad I didn't inherit Mom and Dad's height, the way Laura and Tipper did."

"You can't be both a player and an announcer," Karie said, "and you're going to be a great announcer."

"I hope so." Ginger had wanted to be a sports announcer ever since she could remember. Her parents thought her interest would pass as she got older. Neither of them cared about sports, nor did Laura, so they didn't understand Ginger's determination to be a broadcaster.

Ginger loved to listen to radio broadcasts of sporting events; she liked how the announcers used words to create a picture in the listeners' minds. But she always used a video camera to do her broadcasts. That way when she replayed the tapes at home, she could check to see how closely her descriptions matched the action. She could see only half the court at a time through her viewer, but the school games moved slowly enough that she rarely missed a play.

The game started. Ginger aimed the camera at the basketball court and began her play-by-play description.

The lead seesawed back and forth between the two teams. Despite her promise, Karie was soon yelling like crazy, but Ginger didn't move away from her. She continued speaking softly into the mike.

"Susan Fields carries the ball down court. She pumps, fakes, and passes to Jessica Andrews. Andrews dribbles to the far side and passes back to Fields. Fields is double-teamed. She hands it off to Polly Vaughn, who goes in for the layup. The shot is good, and Roosevelt regains the lead, twenty-two to twenty-one. Rebound by number fourteen for Elk Grove."

At the start of the fourth quarter, the score was tied. Karie said, "So much for Elk Grove being at the bottom of the league."

"It's anybody's game, at this point," Ginger agreed.

The lead continued to flip-flop. With only one minute left, and the score tied, Mr. Wren called a time-out.

Ginger used the break to climb down and stand on the sidelines. As soon as she was on the floor, Ginger used the zoom lens for a close-up of the coach talking to the team. She was close enough to hear his words.

"Concentrate," Mr. Wren said. "Don't let their chatter distract you. You're a great team, and you're going to win this game. All you have to do is—"

Right in the middle of the coach's pep talk, while he

was telling them what strategy to use, Mrs. Vaughn suddenly pushed her way into the huddle.

"When are you going to put Polly back in the game?" she demanded.

Ginger's mouth dropped open in surprise.

"Please sit down, Mrs. Vaughn," Mr. Wren said. "I'll be glad to talk with you after the game."

"We need the starting lineup back in there," Mrs. Vaughn said. "Roosevelt would be winning easily right now if you didn't insist on giving every player equal time."

One of the referees hurried over and said, "I must ask you to return to your seat, ma'am."

Polly got off the bench. "Mom, please," she said. "Don't interfere. Today is my turn to play the first and third quarters."

Mrs. Vaughn ignored Polly. She glared at the referee and stayed where she was. "If the coach can't figure out that the best players are the ones who can win the game, then someone needs to tell him," she said.

"Right on!" yelled a man who was seated behind the Roosevelt players. "You tell him!" A woman sitting beside the man looked embarrassed. She shook her head at the man, and put her finger to her lips.

Ginger recognized the woman. It was Susan Fields's mother.

"You see?" Mrs. Vaughn said. "The other parents agree with me."

"Sit down immediately," the referee said. "Or you will be ejected from this gymnasium."

Mrs. Vaughn huffed back to her seat.

Polly plopped down on the bench and put her head in her hands.

The five players who were in the huddle returned their attention to Mr. Wren just as the buzzer sounded. Ginger climbed back to her place beside Karie.

"Can you believe she did that?" Karie said. "I would crawl under the seats if my mother ever behaved that way."

The game resumed.

Mr. Wren made no substitutions.

Ginger continued her play-by-play. "Roosevelt takes the ball in bounds," Ginger said. "Larson passes to Sumner, who turns, jumps, and shoots. Air ball! It never touched the net. Rebound by number eleven for Elk Grove."

As she talked into the microphone, Ginger heard someone booing.

"Elk Grove shoots, misses, gets the rebound, shoots again. Two points. Forty-nine to forty-seven Elk Grove, with twenty-three seconds left."

"We want the starters. WE WANT THE START-ERS!"

Ginger turned the camera on the crowd and saw angry faces shouting, "WE WANT THE START-ERS!" Mrs. Vaughn was on her feet, leading the chant. Mr. Fields stood beside her, shaking his fist.

The chant became louder as more parents and some students on the Roosevelt side yelled for their best players to return to the game.

Ginger zoomed the camera in on Coach Wren. His jaw was clenched, but his eyes were on the game, not the spectators.

"Go, Roosevelt!" Karie shouted. "Go, Roosevelt!"

"Fifteen seconds left," Ginger said. "It's Roosevelt's ball. Miller dribbles it down the court, fakes to Sumner, and—it's stolen by number eleven for Elk Grove."

More boos erupted.

"Number eleven races down by herself, and sinks the two-pointer. Fifty-one to forty-seven. Elk Grove has the lead with nine seconds remaining on the clock."

"GO, ROOSEVELT!" screamed Karie.

"Beth Sumner takes the ball in for Roosevelt," Ginger said. A whistle blew. "Sumner is called for traveling. Elk Grove gets the ball back with six seconds to go."

The boos got louder. Beth Sumner's mother said angrily, "Those players need encouragement, not boos."

Karie's shoulders slumped. "That's it," she said. "All

Elk Grove has to do is hang on to the ball for six seconds."

Elk Grove not only hung on, they scored another basket.

The final buzzer sounded. "Elk Grove upsets favored Roosevelt," Ginger said into the microphone. "Final score: Elk Grove fifty-three, Roosevelt forty-seven."

"I have to get home," Karie said. "See you tomorrow."

Ginger waved good-bye and kept the camera running as the Roosevelt team congratulated the girls from Elk Grove and Mr. Wren shook hands with Elk Grove's coach.

When Mr. Wren returned to the sidelines, Mrs. Vaughn, Mr. Fields, and two other parents waited for him. One after another, they spoke:

"How can we expect the students to have school pride when the coach doesn't care if his team wins or loses?"

"This isn't kindergarten, you know. Some of these kids will be in high school next year. College scouts will be watching them to see if they're scholarship material."

"It isn't fair to the good players to throw away a game that they could have won."

After listening to the barrage of words for a few minutes, Mr. Wren held up his hand, and the complaints turned to mumbles.

"I know you're disappointed that we lost," he said. "So am I. But my coaching philosophy is that middle school students need playing time, including competitive time during actual games, in order to develop their skills. We are not trying for a world championship here. These kids are twelve, thirteen, and fourteen years old, and the purpose of our sports program is to help them develop physical coordination and self-esteem, and to learn to enjoy playing a team sport. Winning is not and never has been the primary goal. An attitude of good sportsmanship *is* a primary goal, and I would hope that you parents will set a good example for your children."

"You need to enter the real world, Coach," Mrs. Vaughn said. "Children are not helped by being coddled. Pretending that every player is equal in ability doesn't make it so."

"I've never said they have equal ability," Mr. Wren said. "I've said they are equally important, and they will have equal playing time." He picked up his clipboard. "The girls are waiting in the locker room for my postgame comments," he said. "Excuse me." He turned and walked away.

"Don't let them bother you, Coach," came a voice

from partway up the bleachers. "You did a great job!"

Ginger looked to see who was talking, and saw the coach's wife and their four-year-old daughter, Dana. She went to say hello.

"When are you going to baby-sit me again?" Dana asked. "I want to play kickball, like we did last time."

"Ginger will baby-sit when Mommy and Daddy can afford to go somewhere," Mrs. Wren said. "Which won't be soon." Her cheeks were flushed; Ginger could tell she was angry.

"I wish the referee had ejected Mrs. Vaughn," Ginger said.

"Those parents make me furious," Mrs. Wren said. "Bill is a dedicated coach. He truly cares about his players and wants the best for them."

"The kids all like him," Ginger said. "Way more girls went out for basketball this year than in previous years."

"He told the parents and the players his coaching position at the start of the season. They have known since day one that every player will have equal playing time; they all agreed to that when they joined the team."

"Not all the parents are upset," Ginger said.

"No. Just the vocal ones." Mrs. Wren sighed and smiled at Ginger. "I'm sorry," she said. "I shouldn't take out my frustration on you."

"I know a secret," said Dana.

"We don't tell secrets," Mrs. Wren said. "Remember? Secrets are just for our family."

"I know that," Dana said, looking indignant. She lowered her voice and whispered to Ginger, "I'm going to have a baby brother or baby sister."

"Dana!" said Mrs. Wren. "I just told you, that's only for our family to know."

Dana looked surprised. "Ginger's our family," she said. "She baby-sits me."

Ginger laughed. So did Mrs. Wren.

"Congratulations," Ginger said. "I promise I won't tell anyone until you've announced it."

Ginger talked to Mrs. Wren until the gym was empty. Mrs. Wren and Dana went to wait outside the locker room for Mr. Wren.

Ginger walked down the hall to her locker, got her backpack, and started for the door. Her footsteps echoed in the empty hallway. She wondered if the activity bus was still there. If it had already left, she would need to call home and ask for a ride. She lived less than a mile from school, but she was not allowed to walk home alone.

She pushed the door open and stopped.

The bus had already left.

A white car waited in the bus zone.

Chapter Five

GINGER STEPPED BACK INSIDE, pulling the door closed. Was it the same car that had parked in front of the Lawtons' house? Had the driver seen her?

She inhaled deeply, trying to stay calm. There are lots of white cars, she told herself. It's probably some parent, waiting to give his kid a ride home.

She eased the door open an inch and peered out, relieved that no one was coming toward the door. She tried to see who was in the car. A shadowy figure sat behind the wheel, but in the dark interior Ginger could not tell if the driver was a man or a woman.

She noticed a ribbon fluttering from the car's antenna. Had the car at the Lawtons' had a ribbon? If so,

Ginger had not noticed it. It probably isn't the same car at all, she thought. I'm getting all worked into a sweat over nothing.

She went to the pay phone, which hung on the wall just inside the school door, dropped in her coins, and dialed. The line was busy.

She tried again. Still busy.

She cracked open the door and looked out.

The car stayed where it was.

The woman from the restaurant would not park outside the school and wait for me at this time of day, Ginger told herself. She would not know what time I usually leave school. She doesn't know I always stay and tape the basketball practices or the games. Besides, if she wants to find me, she knows where I live. She doesn't need to hang around here.

On her third try, the phone rang. Ten minutes later, Laura arrived, and Ginger ran out to the curb.

"Are you okay?" Laura asked as she drove away. "You sounded kind of funny when you called, as if you were upset about something."

Ginger hesitated. Should she tell Laura her suspicions? What would she say—*There's a white car parked in front of the school so I think someone's watching me?* She would sound like Tipper.

"We lost our game," Ginger said. "And some of the parents got mad at Mr. Wren for not letting the best players stay in the whole time. Queen Victoria actually walked out on the gym floor during a time-out and argued with the coach because he had Polly on the bench."

She looked over her shoulder. The headlights on the white car went on; the car pulled away from the curb.

"I think parents should be banned from attending their offspring's sporting events," Laura said. "I remember when I was on the high school volleyball team, there was one mother who spoiled every game. If anyone made the least little mistake, she yelled at us. And she was always arguing with the referees."

As they talked, Ginger looked back again. The white car turned left at the corner.

"I was glad you called," Laura said. "You can help me talk some sense into Mom and Dad."

"About what?"

"Dad leaves the day after tomorrow for his player piano convention in Atlanta."

"Is that this week? He's talked about it for so long, I had forgotten when it is."

"Well, it starts Wednesday evening. And about an hour ago, Mom got a panicked call from a customer who used to live here and who now lives in Chicago. The customer's daughter has decided to get married on Saturday."

"*This* Saturday? As in five days from now?"

"That's right. The mother's practically hysterical,

and says she can't possibly get ready for the wedding without Mom's help. She's offered to pay Mom's airfare, hotel, and a five-hundred-dollar bonus over and above Mom's regular charge, if Mom will fly to Chicago and help out."

"Is Mom going to do it?"

"She wants to, but she's worried about leaving us alone."

"You're kidding!"

"She is actually considering hiring Mrs. Thomas to come and stay with us."

"A baby-sitter? You're a freshman in college, for pete's sake. And I do baby-sitting myself."

"I think she's worried about Tipper."

"We can handle Tipper," Ginger said.

"That's what I told her."

Ginger was still sputtering when they got home. "If you hire Mrs. Thomas to stay here while you're gone," she told her mother, "I am going to Karie's for the week. And if Karie's mom won't have me, I'll run away and sleep on a park bench."

"You'll do nothing of the kind," Mrs. Shaw said.

"Mrs. Thomas calls me sweetie," Tipper said. "She tries to read baby books to me."

"A sitter would be totally demoralizing," Ginger said. "What would my friends think?"

"They would think we are sensible parents who did not want to leave a six-year-old at home for five days without mature adult supervision."

"I'm a mature adult," Laura said.

"If you have a sitter stay here," Ginger said, "it will ruin my reputation forever."

"Maybe I can stay with Marcus," Tipper suggested.

"I don't trust you to behave yourself for five days with Marcus," Mrs. Shaw said. "The two of you will drive his mother crazy."

"I'll be good. I promise! Please, Mom? Call Marcus's mother and see if I can go there. Then when his parents go somewhere, Marcus can stay here."

"That's a good solution," Mr. Shaw said. "If Tipper stays with Marcus, the girls can manage on their own."

The comment surprised Ginger. When it came to family matters, Dad usually let Mom make the decisions, and he went along with whatever she thought.

"Well . . . " Mrs. Shaw said. "It would be a challenge to go to Chicago and put together a wedding on such short notice."

Tipper picked up the telephone, dialed Marcus's number, and handed the phone to Mrs. Shaw. Then he crossed all his fingers, crossed his legs, and crossed his eyes.

Marcus's mother said she would be delighted to

have Tipper come. "It's no harder to watch two of them than to watch one," she said.

Tipper shouted, "We can work on our burping lessons!" He ran into his room and began throwing the toys he wanted to take with him into a brown paper grocery bag.

"Call your customer and tell her you're coming," Laura said.

Quick, Ginger thought, before you change your mind about Mrs. Thomas.

The rest of the evening was spent in a flurry of preparations. Mrs. Shaw made a plane reservation for Wednesday morning and changed her appointments for the rest of the week. Ginger did her homework and helped Tipper condense what he was taking to Marcus's house to a total of three grocery bags.

"Someone called for you after school," Tipper said.

"Who?"

"She didn't say her name. It was a grown-up, and she was rude. She asked what time you would be home, and I told her you usually stay to watch basketball practice. She hung up without saying thank you or good-bye."

Tipper tried to stuff his radio-controlled car into the bag. It tore the paper, all the toys spilled out, and he and Ginger had to start over with a new bag.

While they worked, questions bounced in Ginger's mind like tennis balls at a tournament. Was the white car at school the same car that had been parked at the Lawtons'? Was the driver the woman from the restaurant?

Is she following me? Ginger wondered. Watching me? Did she call here to find out what time I get home from school—and then, when she learned I stay for basketball practice, did she wait for me outside the school?

Or is my imagination working double-time?

She said nothing about her suspicions to her parents. If they knew she was worried, they'd hire Mrs. Thomas for sure. Or, more likely, one of them would stay home.

Before she went to bed, Ginger went out to her dad's workshop. "You listen to a lot of mystery books on tape," she said. "I'm wondering, if a character thinks someone is following him, what does the character usually do?"

"They change their appearance," Mr. Shaw said. "They shave their beards or dye their hair a different color or stuff a pillow inside their clothes. Why? Are you writing a mystery?"

"I'm thinking about one," Ginger said.

"Good!" Mr. Shaw said. "You can become a famous

writer and support your dear father in his old age."

Ginger lay in bed and thought about how she could change her appearance. She knew that because of a teachers' conference school would get out early the next day. She decided to spend the afternoon giving herself a new look.

Chapter Six

GINGER SCOWLED AT HERSELF in the bathroom mirror. Her hair didn't look at all the way she had hoped it would. Maybe I should have gone to Fast Clips, she thought, instead of cutting it myself.

It had seemed like a good idea to change her hairstyle so that if the woman sat outside school, looking for Ginger, she would be less likely to recognize her. But Ginger had not intended to change the style so drastically.

She put the scissors back in the drawer and walked from the bathroom to the kitchen. She watched Laura take a cookie sheet filled with tiny butter cookies out of the oven.

"Hi," Ginger said.

Laura did not look up. "Can you be my helper tonight?" she asked as she used a spatula to lift the cookies onto a wire cooling rack. "Queen Victoria is having a reception for a pianist who's giving a concert in Seattle tomorrow, and I'm desperate for someone to help pass the cheese balls."

"I have a student council meeting at seven. What time is the party?"

"The guests don't come until eight, but I need to be there by . . ." Laura looked up and stopped in midsentence. "What happened to your hair?" she said.

"I cut it."

"I can see that." Laura wrinkled up her nose, as if Ginger's hair smelled bad. "It's only two inches long!"

"Two and a half," Ginger said.

"It's so shaggy! What did you use, the garden shears?"

"I used Mom's manicure scissors." You would think I had stabbed someone with them, Ginger thought, the way she's acting.

"Why didn't you go to a hair salon? Why on earth would you do it yourself?"

"I don't like hair salons," Ginger said. "The stylists always ask me how I want my hair cut, and I don't know what to say. They're the experts. Why do they ask me what they should do?"

"Just say you want a trim," Laura said.

Sure, Ginger thought. A trim. In other words, have them cut it exactly the same way they cut it the last time and the time before that and the time before that. And I will look the same as I have always looked.

Ginger didn't want to look the way she always looked. That was the whole point. In the past, whenever the person in the hair salon draped that plastic cape around her shoulders and asked how she wanted her hair cut, what she had really wanted to say was, "Cut it so I look gorgeous. Make me so beautiful that every boy in the eighth grade will be hanging around my locker." Instead, Ginger always shrugged and mumbled, "I don't care."

This time, Ginger wanted to change the way she looked for a different reason, but she didn't tell Laura that. Instead she said, "I saved fourteen dollars by cutting my hair myself."

"Next time ask Mom for the fourteen dollars." Laura began cutting the crusts off a loaf of French bread. "She would gladly spend the money to keep you from looking like a freak."

"For your information," Ginger said, "this haircut is practical, stylish, and not at all freaky."

Tipper catapulted through the back door, wearing his cowboy outfit. He stopped in front of Ginger. "Cool," he said. "You look like those weird people we saw downtown who had rings in their belly buttons."

"I rest my case," said Laura.

"What does he know about hairstyles?" Ginger said. "He's had a cowboy hat on his head ever since he was born."

"I like your hair this way," Tipper said. "Remember that one guy we saw who had half his hair purple and the other half orange? I liked his hair, too." Tipper took a drink of water and then let out a loud belch.

"Out!" Laura said, pointing to the door.

"I'm practicing my teaching methods," Tipper said.

"Is Polly Vaughn on student council?" Laura asked.

"No. She ran for it but she didn't get elected."

"I'll call Polly Vaughn," Laura said, "and see if she can help me. That way, you won't have to leave your meeting early."

Ginger returned to the bathroom. She stared at her reflection, knowing Laura was right. The haircut was terrible; she did look like a freak. She wondered if she could wear a stocking hat pulled down over her ears for a few months.

Probably not.

She had not intended to cut off so much hair. She wanted to change how she looked, but not this way. The sides had kept coming out uneven, so she kept snipping, and her hair got shorter and shorter, and then it was too late.

Ginger went into her parents' bedroom and picked up the telephone. When Karie answered, Ginger said, "I need to warn you. I cut my hair."

"I had mine cut today, too," Karie said. "It doesn't look much different, though. I only got a trim."

"Mine looks different."

"Oh, good. I love new hairstyles. Where did you have it done?"

"In the bathroom. I cut it myself."

There was a slight pause. "How does it look?" Karie said.

"Tipper says I remind him of some people we saw who had rings in their navels."

"That bad, huh?"

"It's short. *Really* short."

"How short?" Karie asked. "Exactly."

"About two inches. Everywhere."

"Two inches?" Karie squeaked. "What did your mom say?"

"She hasn't seen me yet, but Laura threw a fit. You know how she is about appearances, always worrying what people might think. She was begging me to help her serve a party tonight, and then when she saw my hair she changed her mind."

"Maybe it isn't as bad as you think," Karie said.

"Thanks. I have to hang up; I just heard Mom come home."

"See you at the student council meeting."

"Do you know what the meeting is about?"

"Nope. All I know is Nancy Randolph called a special emergency meeting, and she said it's important."

Two hours later, Ginger went into the gym for the meeting. Karie ran to greet her. She walked all around Ginger, looking at the front and back of her head.

"It's cute," Karie said, sounding surprised. "It *is* short, but it's classy looking. I like it."

"Thanks," Ginger said.

"From the way you talked on the phone, I was prepared to see a real hatchet job."

"It was," Ginger said. "You are seeing me *after* Mom spent thirty-two dollars, plus a five-dollar tip, for a stylist at The Velvet Kitten to—and I quote my mother—'fix this mess.' "

"Oh," said Karie. "Well, it looks good now. You were lucky they could take you at The Velvet Kitten on such short notice."

"Mom pleaded. She's leaving for Chicago in the morning, and she said I had to look decent before she left. The stylist knows Mom because Mom refers a lot of brides to The Velvet Kitten for their wedding-day hairdos."

Nancy held up her hand. Everyone quit talking and found seats. "I called an emergency meeting because a petition has been filed with the school board to fire Mr. Wren as coach of the girls' basketball team."

Gasps of surprise intermingled with shocked comments.

"Why?"

"What happened?"

"Who wants him fired?"

"The formal request came from Mrs. Vaughn."

Ginger and Karie glanced at each other. "That figures," Ginger said.

Nancy continued. "The petition states that Mr. Wren is unfit for the job of girls' basketball coach and cites four reasons:

1. His unwillingness to recognize which players are most capable.

2. His inability to teach basketball skills.

3. His inadequate strategy during games."

"That is totally ridiculous," said Karie.

"Unfortunately," Nancy said, "a few other parents support Mrs. Vaughn. They claim that they were never told at the start of the season about his plan to give everyone equal playing time."

"That isn't true," Beth Sumner said. "He told all of

us when we tried out, and he told us again at the first practice. I thought it was great because I knew I'd probably sit on the bench all season if he only put the best players in the games."

"What's the fourth reason?" asked Ginger.

"The petition also charges that the practice sessions are unorganized and do not teach any practical skills."

"What?" cried Susan Fields. "He's the best coach in the league! I've learned more from him in one season than I knew about basketball my whole life before this year."

"The school board is holding a preliminary hearing tomorrow night at seven o'clock," Nancy said. "I think the student council should attend and voice our support for Mr. Wren."

The vote was unanimous.

After the meeting, Ginger waited for her mom to pick her up. She looked carefully around the parking lot, relieved that no white car was parked outside.

The woman could not have known about an unscheduled meeting, Ginger thought. Normally Ginger stayed home on Tuesday nights.

When Mrs. Shaw arrived Ginger said, "If I never see Mrs. Vaughn again, it will be fine with me. She's trying to get Mr. Wren fired as basketball coach."

"I know," Mrs. Shaw said. "She called this afternoon and asked me to sign her petition."

"Did you?"

"No, I didn't," her mother replied. "It was hard to refuse because Mrs. Vaughn gives Laura and me so much business, but I don't know anything about the basketball team."

"I do. Mr. Wren is a good coach and a great social studies teacher," Ginger said. "He's in charge of the Natural Helpers program, and he always chaperons the Saturday field trips, and if kids have a problem, they know they can go to Mr. Wren for help and he won't act like it's all the kid's fault for being in trouble."

"Mrs. Vaughn seems convinced he should be replaced. I suspect she called everyone she knows who has a student at Roosevelt. She wants a crowd at the school board hearing. I told her my husband and I were both leaving town tomorrow morning."

"The student council is going to the meeting to support Mr. Wren," Ginger said.

"Be careful what you say. Mrs. Vaughn can be vindictive."

"What do you mean?"

"She doesn't have to hire B.A. Catering for her parties, or recommend Celebrations to her friends. Laura and I get a lot of business because Mrs. Vaughn likes us and our work."

"She's wrong about Mr. Wren," Ginger said.

They rode the rest of the way home in silence.

When Ginger got home, Tipper told her, "That lady called again."

"Did you get her name this time?"

"No. She asked what time you go to school in the morning. I told her seven-thirty, but you might leave early tomorrow because Mom and Dad are going out of town."

"Oh, Tipper," Mrs. Shaw scolded. "You must never tell a stranger that your parents are away."

Tipper looked surprised. "Was she a stranger?" he asked. "I thought she was someone Ginger baby-sits for."

My baby-sitting customers always leave their names, Ginger thought, and their phone numbers.

Chapter Seven

JOYCE TOOK THE LAST load of laundry out of the dryer, carefully folding each piece of clothing. There. Everything was clean and ready to pack.

She wondered what size the girl wore. She wouldn't have any extra clothing with her when she and Joyce left.

Maybe she can wear my clothes, Joyce thought. If not, I'll buy her new clothes. We'll have to get rid of the ones she's wearing when we leave. Even though she'll come willingly this time, someone may try to find her.

. . .

Ginger woke up before her alarm went off. She felt anxious, as if she'd had a bad dream, but she could not recall what it was. Then she remembered the white car, and the woman who called and asked what time Ginger got home and what time she left for school.

Ginger smelled coffee and heard voices in the kitchen. She looked at her clock. Five-fifty.

She got up and pulled the curtain away from the bedroom window. Heavy mist dampened the gray predawn light.

There was no white car, but the blue and yellow Super Shuttle was parked in front of the house. She knew that Mom and Dad were leaving for the airport at six o'clock. She put on her bathrobe and went out to say good-bye. Laura slouched on the sofa, half asleep. Tipper, in his cowboy outfit, galloped around the room.

Mr. and Mrs. Shaw had already carried out their luggage. They hugged Ginger, Laura, and Tipper, gave them some last-minute instructions, and climbed aboard.

"Bring me a present!" Tipper called.

"I'm going back to bed," Laura said. Yawning, she left the room.

Ginger watched the shuttle's taillights slide into the fog. She looked forward to being on her own with Laura, but she wished it hadn't happened right when a strange woman was calling and asking about Ginger's schedule. She looked both ways into the mist and saw only the empty street. Shivering, she went inside and locked the door behind her.

Tipper sat at the kitchen table eating a bowl of Cheerios.

Ginger got a pitcher and began mixing a can of frozen orange juice.

Tipper set his empty bowl in the dishwasher. He put on his coat.

"What are you doing?" Ginger said. "It's only six A.M., and it's raining."

"I'm going to Marcus's house."

"You can't go over there now."

"Why not?"

"It's too early."

"Mom and Dad have left. I'm supposed to stay with Marcus while they're gone. Two kids are signed up for burping lessons on Saturday, and we need to get ready."

"Laura will take you to Marcus's house after school today," Ginger said. "It's all arranged with Marcus's mother."

Tipper took off his coat. "You should have told me last night that I wasn't going to Marcus's until after school," he said. "I got up at five-thirty for nothing."

Ginger poured herself a glass of juice.

Tipper took his bowl out of the dishwasher and

filled it with more Cheerios. This time, he didn't put milk on them. He munched them dry, using his fingers instead of a spoon.

"You know the day when I asked if you saw who was driving that white car?" Ginger said.

Tipper nodded.

"Did you see who it was, or didn't you?"

"It wasn't really a cute guy with a sign. I made that up."

"Thanks a lot."

"It was that same lady who talked to us at your birthday party."

Ginger set her glass down. "When we were in the restaurant?"

"Right." Tipper chomped another handful of Cheerios.

"Why didn't you tell me?" Ginger said.

"I wanted to make Marcus laugh."

"I wouldn't have asked you about the driver if it wasn't important," Ginger said. "Are you certain it was the same woman?"

"Yes. She was crying."

"Crying? Are you sure?"

Tipper nodded. "Marcus and I were playing catch in the street, and we stepped on the curb to let the white car go by, and when she went past me, I saw that the lady was crying. And so I looked closer, and that's when I remembered seeing her before, when she came over and told you 'happy birthday.' "

So it *was* her, Ginger thought. She did follow us home. She sat there and watched our house. And she followed Laura to Mrs. Vaughn's house and went to the party and took Laura's business card.

"Did you notice anything else?" Ginger asked. "Anything about the car?"

"Like what?"

"Sometimes a car will have a funny bumper sticker."

Tipper shook his head.

"Or it will have something hanging from the rear-view mirror, like a crystal or a pair of dice."

"No. I didn't see anything like that."

"Or it will have something on the antenna," Ginger continued, "so the owner can pick out the car quickly in a parking lot."

"It had a ribbon," Tipper said.

"On the antenna?"

"Yes. A yellow ribbon."

"You should have told me the truth when I asked you," Ginger said, "instead of showing off for Marcus."

"Who is she?" Tipper asked.

"I don't know."

"Is she a spy?" Tipper's eyes grew round. "Are you going to call the police?"

Ginger knew better than to tell her brother that she

suspected she was being followed. Tipper would make up a million theories about why someone was spying on Ginger, and he would blab them to everyone he knew.

"She is not a spy," Ginger said.

"Maybe you do have a boyfriend," Tipper said, "and that lady is his mother. She wants to know what sort of girl her son is in love with, so she sneaks over here and watches you."

"Give me a break," said Ginger.

Tipper grinned at her. "That would explain why she was crying," he said.

"Very funny." Ginger finished her glass of juice. "If you see her again," she said, "let me know."

Tipper burped.

As she dressed for school, Ginger thought about Mr. Wren and his future as a coach. Ginger got along well with all of her teachers, but Mr. Wren was her favorite. He had been, ever since the day Bugs died.

Bugs had been Ginger's first house rabbit. He was a soft gray bunny who quickly learned to use a litter pan. Bugs used to nuzzle his nose against Ginger's ankles, asking her to pet him. He followed her around so much that Ginger's dad said she should have named him Shadow.

Last fall, when Bugs was four years old, Tipper accidentally left the front door open. Usually Ginger kept

Bugs confined in her room but he had been hopping free in the house that morning, and he ventured outside. A neighbor's dog—part Rottweiler and part Doberman—caught Bugs and shook him, breaking the rabbit's neck.

It happened early in the morning; Ginger buried Bugs before she left for school. She had thought she could make it through the day, but when she got to her first-period class, which Mr. Wren taught, and started to tell Karie what had happened, she burst into tears.

Mr. Wren took Ginger to a small private room that was reserved for teachers only. "Stay as long as you like," he told her. "Go ahead and cry. You need to grieve for your little friend."

Later Ginger told Karie, "Mr. Wren never once said, 'It was only a rabbit' or 'You can always get another pet.' Instead, he said Bugs must have been a very special rabbit for me to love him so much. He said I should remember all the fun times I had with Bugs, and cherish my memories."

As Ginger remembered Mr. Wren's kindness, she decided it was the very trait that Mrs. Vaughn objected to. Because Mr. Wren cared about all the players, not just the star athletes, he was faced with losing his job as coach. It wasn't fair.

While Ginger waited for the school bus, a white car approached. She immediately looked at the antenna;

there was no yellow ribbon attached. Even so, she stepped back from the curb until the car passed. The driver was a young man, with a baby strapped in a car seat.

When Ginger got off the bus at school she glanced quickly around. A steady string of cars snaked in and out of the school's driveway as parents dropped off their children. She had never realized before how many cars are white.

All day, Ginger felt edgy. After school, she decided to tape the boys' basketball game. Although the game was close, Ginger left before the final buzzer because she wanted to be sure to catch the activity bus. With Mom and Dad away, she couldn't count on getting a ride home—and she certainly didn't want to walk home alone. Not this week.

When she opened the door, she saw a white car in the school lot, where the driver had a good view of the front door. A ribbon hung from the antenna.

Maybe she won't recognize me with my hair short, Ginger thought, but immediately she knew that was silly. Everyone at school today had known who she was. Cutting her hair to fool the woman had been a stupid idea.

Ginger was tempted to go over to the car and confront the driver. But what could she say? Stop following me? Quit watching me? She had no proof that the woman was waiting for her.

As Ginger started toward the bus, the woman got out of her car and came toward Ginger. "I need to talk to you," she said.

"About what?"

Ginger knew all the rules about screaming and running away if she was ever threatened by a stranger. But this woman was small, not much bigger than Ginger herself, and she did not appear to have any kind of weapon. She didn't try to touch Ginger, or even come closer to her. She stood still, her empty hands at her sides, and spoke softly.

"Not here. In private." She smiled at Ginger, a tender, loving smile. "It's important."

"Who are you?"

"I'll drive you home. We can talk in the car."

"No. If it's so important, you can call my parents and arrange a time to see me."

"Your parents are out of town."

A shiver tingled down the back of Ginger's neck. It *was* this woman who had called.

The bus engine started.

"I have to go," Ginger said. She walked past the woman and boarded the bus, her heart racing. She took the backseat and watched out the rear window. As the bus pulled into the street, the car drove away, too, but it did not follow the bus.

She doesn't need to follow the bus, Ginger thought. She already knows where I live. She knows my name and address and telephone number. She knows my daily schedule and she knows my parents are away. But I don't know anything about her.

What if she drives to my house and waits for me as I walk home from the bus?

The bus had to wait at the railroad crossing while a slow freight train lumbered past. Hurry up, Ginger thought. I want to get home before she arrives.

The car was not waiting when the bus reached Ginger's corner, nor was it parked anywhere on Ginger's street. Relieved, Ginger trotted home.

Laura looked up from the book she was reading. "You just had a phone call," she said, "from a very impolite woman."

"What did she say?"

"When I answered, she thought I was you. She said, 'Hello, Ginger. I'm so glad you answered.' But when I said, 'Ginger isn't home yet; this is Laura,' she hung up. Slammed the receiver down, right in my ear."

"Did you recognize the voice?"

"She sounded kind of familiar, but I don't know why."

"I do," Ginger said. "You heard her wish me a

happy birthday in the restaurant, and later you talked to her at Mrs. Vaughn's party."

"What are you talking about?"

"That woman waited for me outside school today. She said she needs to talk to me. I told her she would have to speak to Mom and Dad first."

Laura frowned at Ginger. "Who is she?"

"I have no idea. The first time I saw her was that day in the restaurant, but she looks at me as if I'm her dearest friend. It's creepy."

"I'm going to call Mom."

"And make her come home? I'll tell Mom and Dad as soon as they get back. If the woman calls again, hang up."

"I don't like this," Laura said.

"I don't like it, either, but I don't want to ruin Dad's convention and the wedding Mom's supervising. All the woman did was ask to talk to me. It isn't as if she tried to grab me or something."

"If she comes to school again, tell a teacher."

Ginger nodded. She was certain the woman would show up again. The only question was when. And why.

Joyce Enderly wrote down what she would say to the girl, once they were alone. She wouldn't be nervous if she had practiced her speech ahead of time. She went over it in her head, wanting it to be perfect. The girl wasn't as easily persuaded as she had been when she was ten years old—back when she was Lisa. Joyce would have to be careful to say everything exactly right. She might not get another chance if the girl got scared off again, like she had in Montana.

The girl. Why do I keep calling her "the girl"? Joyce thought, and then knew it was because she didn't like the name, Ginger. *I* would never have named her Ginger, Joyce thought. Well, once I get her away from here, we can talk about changing her name.

Melissa. Yes, Melissa would be nice. I've always wanted a daughter named Melissa.

Chapter Eight

KARIE'S DAD DROVE KARIE and Ginger to the school board hearing. It was held in the school district's administration building, directly across the street from Roosevelt School.

"I'm going to come in and listen," Mr. Bradley said. "I was impressed by Mr. Wren at the parents' open house last fall. And I don't like it when someone uses a position of authority in business to manipulate private lives."

"What do you mean?" Karie asked.

"I heard a lot of talk at work today about what Mrs. Vaughn is trying to do."

Ginger knew that Karie's dad worked for a large

advertising agency. She wondered why employees of an ad agency would be talking about the girls' basketball coach.

"What kind of talk?" Karie asked.

"She is pressuring people who do business with Vaughn Enterprises to take her side in this. I happened to be in George Randolph's office when she called him."

"Nancy Randolph's dad?"

"Vaughn Billboards is George's biggest client," Mr. Bradley said. "She didn't come right out and threaten to take the Vaughn business to another agency, but she strongly suggested that George show up tonight and speak against Mr. Wren."

"Is he going to?"

"I don't know."

"Nancy Randolph is talking on behalf of the student council," Karie told her dad, "in favor of keeping Mr. Wren as coach."

"That puts George between a rock and a hard place, doesn't it?" Mr. Bradley said.

He isn't the only one, Ginger thought. I'd like to speak in favor of keeping Mr. Wren, but I don't want Mom and Laura to lose Mrs. Vaughn's business.

"The word around the office," Mr. Bradley said, "was that Mrs. Vaughn made similar pressure calls to other people."

A notice outside the meeting room directed anyone who wanted to speak at the meeting to sign up in advance and limit their remarks to three minutes. THIS IS A PRELIMINARY HEARING, the notice said. THERE WILL BE ANOTHER OPPORTUNITY FOR PUBLIC OPINION AT THE FINAL HEARING ON FRIDAY AT SIX P.M.

Ginger and Karie read the names of the people who had signed up to speak. Mrs. Vaughn was first, followed by three parents whose daughters played on the basketball team. Nancy was next.

Mr. Bradley read the list over their shoulders. "I don't see George's name," he said.

"Maybe there will be so many people in favor of keeping Mr. Wren that the whole thing will get called off," Karie said.

"Don't count on it," said Karie's dad. "When Victoria Vaughn wants something, she usually gets it."

They found seats and listened as the formal complaint was read by Mr. Hixler, the president of the school board. Mr. Wren stared straight ahead; Mrs. Wren wiped tears from her eyes. Ginger wondered who was taking care of Dana.

When it was Mrs. Vaughn's turn to speak, she devoted the whole three minutes to her claim that Mr. Wren was an incompetent coach who did not teach his team basketball skills. "The practices," she said, "are loosely run social events with no discipline and no planned drills. The coach's four-year-old daughter is allowed to play on the sidelines, creating a distraction."

"Once!" Mrs. Wren burst out. "Once, when I had the flu and we couldn't get a sitter, Bill took Dana to practice with him."

"Quiet, please," said Mr. Hixler. "Mrs. Vaughn has the floor."

"As for his coaching strategy during actual games," Mrs. Vaughn said, "the Roosevelt record of two wins and six losses speaks for itself."

Someone behind Ginger muttered, "Winning isn't everything."

To Ginger's dismay, the next three speakers echoed Mrs. Vaughn's opinions. All had daughters on the team. Ginger recognized them as the group who had been so angry during the Elk Grove game.

"It's interesting," Karie whispered to Ginger, "that the parents who are on Mrs. Vaughn's side are here alone; their kids stayed home."

"They probably disagree," Ginger said. "I've never heard a single player complain about Mr. Wren."

"I wonder if Polly Vaughn came," Karie said. "I don't see her."

Ginger looked around the room. Her glance swept past rows of kids she knew and adults she didn't know. All the seats were taken, and about a dozen people stood at the back of the room. Ginger looked at them and froze.

The woman stood just inside the door. When Ginger looked at her, the woman smiled. Ginger turned around, her thoughts racing. Maybe the woman is the mother of someone at Roosevelt. Maybe she wants to talk to me about some problem her kid is having at school.

Nancy Randolph was the first student to speak. When she stood up, Mr. Bradley whispered, "That's her dad sitting with her."

"Mr. Wren does teach basketball skills," Nancy said. "He also teaches good sportsmanship, and team spirit, and empathy for your fellow players. I think those qualities are more important than winning."

Nancy's voice grew louder and more confident. "Mr. Wren prepares his players to excel in many ways. Instead of having the narrow focus of Winning Is Everything, he puts sports in perspective and tells his players it is most important to fully develop their talents, and to live up to their highest ideals. If the school board removes Mr. Wren as coach, you will be setting a terrible example for the students. As president of the student council, I speak for the six representatives of each grade. We voted unanimously to oppose firing Mr. Wren."

Applause rang out as Nancy took her seat. Mrs. Vaughn glared at Nancy's father, but Mr. Randolph ignored her and kept clapping.

"I admire George's courage," Mr. Bradley said.

The next speaker, Mrs. Sumner, said, "Beth never used to like sports because the teams were too competitive. With Mr. Wren as coach the game is fun, and that's how it's supposed to be."

"If a student wants to play only for fun," said the next speaker, "she can put together a game with her friends. School should be preparation for real life, and in real life you have to compete. If losing doesn't matter to you, you'll never be successful."

Several students, and some parents, spoke in favor of keeping Mr. Wren. Ginger tried to concentrate on each of the speeches, but her attention wandered to the woman at the back of the room.

She turned to look again; the woman was still staring at her. The woman motioned with one finger for Ginger to come to her. Ginger shook her head no. The woman scowled and motioned more emphatically.

I'm going to talk to her, Ginger decided. When the meeting ends, I'll ask who she is and what she wants. This is a good time to do it, with a crowd of people around. I can't go on like this, constantly looking for her, suspicious of every white car, nervous that I'm being watched.

The last two speakers supported Mrs. Vaughn.

"She's clever," Mr. Bradley said. "She made sure the last speakers were from her side, so those remarks are what people take away with them."

When the meeting ended, Ginger hurried to the back of the room, determined to find out who the woman was.

The woman was gone.

Ginger couldn't believe it. The woman had acted as if it was the most important thing in the world for Ginger to talk to her, and now that Ginger was willing to do it, the woman had left. She is the most bizarre person I've ever seen, Ginger thought. And I wonder where she'll show up next.

Chapter Nine

"I'M AFRAID MRS. VAUGHN might win," Karie said as they left the meeting.

"Mr. Wren needs proof that he is a good coach," Mr. Bradley said. "His supporters talk about coaching philosophy and team spirit, but those things are difficult to measure. When Mrs. Vaughn says Mr. Wren does not teach basketball skills she has the win-loss record as evidence. Everything else is just opinion."

"Some players testified that the practices included drills," Karie said.

"And some parents testified that their kids learned nothing."

"Those were the parents who were angry because

their kids got taken out during the game against Elk Grove," Ginger said.

"That group is like a hurricane," Karie said, "getting louder and more destructive by the hour."

"I don't see why Mrs. Vaughn even cares," Ginger said. "Polly has never complained when she's taken out of a game."

"Last year, Mrs. Vaughn ran for a seat on the city council," Mr. Bradley said. "Mr. Wren campaigned for her opponent, and Mrs. Vaughn lost the election by a large number. I suspect her determination to get him fired is about that election as much as about basketball. Some people can't stand to lose."

Laura was not home when Ginger arrived. Mr. Bradley waited until Ginger had unlocked the door and was safely inside before he drove off, but the house seemed empty and far too quiet.

A note from Laura said, *I went to the library. Will try to get back before you do. If not, I'll be home soon.*

Ginger wandered restlessly around, with Flopsy hopping at her heels. You wanted less commotion, Ginger told herself, and now that you have it, you don't like it.

The trouble, she knew, was not so much that she missed her parents, and she certainly did not miss Tipper's chatter. The trouble was her anxiety over the strange woman, and her concern for Mr. Wren.

Ginger filled Flopsy's food bowl with rabbit kibble, cleaned out his litter box, and put fresh water in his water bottle. As she worked, she remembered what Mrs. Wren had said to Dana about not being able to afford a baby-sitter, or a night out.

Teachers get paid extra for coaching, Ginger knew. The Wrens probably need that income, especially now that they were going to have another baby.

Ginger picked up Flopsy and stroked his fur. She knew Mr. Wren taught his players specific skills. She had seen him do so dozens of times while she was at the gym, practicing to be a sports announcer. If only she could prove it.

Flopsy began wiggling; Ginger put him on the floor. She went into the family room and looked at the boxes of piano rolls on the shelves. She chose a march; something lively would make the house seem more occupied.

She opened the player piano, put the paper roll in place, and began pumping on the foot pedals. The piano keys moved up and down as the piano played "Stars and Stripes Forever." When the song was finished, Ginger rewound the roll and chose another march, "Under the Double Eagle."

Playing the player piano always made her happy. She enjoyed reading the lyrics as the rolls scrolled around, and she liked to push the controls to make the song play loud or soft, fast or slow. She decided not to tell Laura that the woman had come to the meeting. There was no point in worrying Laura when nothing had happened. Ginger pumped the piano until Laura got home.

"How did the school board meeting go?" Laura asked.

"Not well. The Queen is pressuring everyone she knows to speak against Mr. Wren."

"I know," Laura said. "She called me this afternoon."

"What did she say?"

"I wasn't here, but she left a message on the machine. She said she knew my sister was interested in sports and hoped you would want to improve Roosevelt's basketball program by getting a coach who is better qualified than Mr. Wren."

"There are no coaches who are better than Mr. Wren."

Laura continued. "She also said that she hoped she could continue to do business with B.A. Catering."

"In other words, if I don't try to help her get Mr. Wren fired, you lose Mrs. Vaughn's business."

"I'm not sure she would really do it."

"But what if she does?"

"If she does, I'll lose at least half my business. The Queen is a pain, but she's my biggest customer, and she recommends me to all her friends. I have a feeling she would quickly unrecommend me."

"She isn't a queen," Ginger said. "She's a dictator."

"She could make Mom lose business, too."

Ginger knew that her parents paid half of Laura's college expenses, and Laura earned the other half herself. If both Celebrations and B.A. Catering lost a lot of business, the financial impact would be substantial.

"Grandpa and Grandma called after you left," Laura said. "They said they got lonesome for us last night, so they watched the anniversary video again. They said to tell you hi."

And that's when Ginger remembered. Last fall, her family had made a video for the fiftieth anniversary of her dad's parents. Each family member had told the elder Shaws, on tape, about hobbies and recent activities.

For her part of the tape, Ginger had put together a demonstration of herself "broadcasting" a basketball game. In order to make it, she had saved some of her practice videos and then used parts of each, splicing them together.

After finishing the project for her grandparents, she had never erased those tapes or used them over again. She thought they were still in the back of her closet, along with her menu collection and the shoe box full of old valentines. If so, she just might have some footage that would help Mr. Wren.

"I have a history paper to write," Laura said. "I'll be in Mom's office, using the computer."

Ginger put the piano rolls away and closed the piano. Then she searched through everything on the floor of her bedroom closet. She found the videotapes in a plastic grocery bag, under her tennis racket.

She pulled a video out of the bag and looked at the Post-it note that was stuck on it. *Girls' basketball practice, Nov. 21.* Ginger stuck the video in the VCR and punched the Play button.

Two minutes into the film, it showed Mr. Wren teaching his players a drill to improve their layup shots and their rebounding skills. He also explained the proper way to shoot a free throw.

Ginger's excitement grew. This was the proof that Mr. Wren needed.

There were two more tapes. Ginger fast-forwarded through the parts where the girls actually played basketball and watched anything where Mr. Wren talked to the team. All of the tapes showed Mr. Wren teaching his players to play better basketball.

At the end of the third tape, she turned off the VCR, knowing she had a huge decision to make.

She could keep her tapes to herself—and take a

chance that Mr. Wren would lose his coaching job. Or she could turn the tapes over to the school board—and take a chance that Laura would not have enough money to stay in college.

Be loyal to her favorite teacher—or be loyal to her family.

She slept fitfully, waking often. Each time she woke, she lay in the dark thinking about Mr. Wren.

And about the tapes.

And about the woman who kept following her.

Once she tried telling her subconscious to come up with a solution to her problems while she slept. She had watched a talk show program where the guest claimed that anytime he needed guidance, or the answer to a question, he simply directed his subconscious to provide it while he slept, and when he woke up he always had the answer, and knew what he should do.

It didn't work for Ginger. When her alarm went off the next morning she was just as confused and upset as she had been when she went to bed.

She lay there awhile considering her options. Without meaning to, she dozed off. She awoke with a start half an hour later and had to rush through breakfast. She didn't even have time to pack a lunch; she would have to buy a cafeteria lunch.

She hurried to the bus stop. Usually Eric Konen caught the bus at Ginger's corner, but that morning

Eric wasn't there. Ginger looked at her watch, wondering if she had missed the bus. No, she still had four minutes to spare.

While she waited she took her hairbrush out of her backpack and brushed what was left of her hair. She had skipped her usual shower, and she felt unkempt.

"Hello, Ginger."

The sudden soft voice behind her startled her; Ginger had not heard anyone approach. She whirled around.

The woman stood a few feet away.

"Who are you?" Ginger asked.

"I need to talk to you."

"I was going to talk to you after the meeting last night, but you had left."

"There were too many people. Crowds make me nervous."

"What do you want?"

"Will you meet me after school? I have something important to tell you."

"Like what?"

"Not here. This isn't the place, and there isn't enough time before your bus comes. Meet me after school, in the parking lot. We'll go somewhere quiet, where we can talk."

"No," Ginger said.

"It won't take long," the woman said. "If you don't

want to leave the school grounds, we can sit in my car and talk."

"I can't do that," Ginger said. "I don't know you."

A look of pain shot across the woman's face. "Oh, but you do," she whispered. "You do know me; you just don't remember."

Ginger glanced down the street, hoping to see the bus approach. Although she did not feel in any physical danger, the odd conversation and the peculiar look in the woman's eyes made her uneasy.

"I don't know who you are or what you want," Ginger said, "but if you keep following me, I'm going to call the police."

"I didn't mean to upset you. I've been waiting for a chance to speak to you, but you're hardly ever alone. When you are by yourself you get on the bus before I can talk to you. Please say you'll meet me after school."

"No," Ginger said. "If you want to tell me something, you had better do it right here and now."

The woman looked around, as if fearing that someone was hiding nearby, eavesdropping.

"The bus will be here any minute," Ginger said. "Once I get on it, I am not going to talk to you again."

"I didn't plan it this way, standing here on the street. Ever since I saw you in the restaurant on your birthday, and realized who you were, I've been planning how to tell you. I wanted to do it in a cozy tea-room, or on a bench in the city rose garden."

Tears puddled in the woman's eyes. "Please meet me after school," she said. "Please."

The woman's emotion made Ginger even more nervous. She shook her head.

The yellow school bus turned the corner, two blocks away, and rumbled toward them. Relieved, Ginger stepped toward the curb.

"Ginger," the woman said.

Ginger looked at her.

"Please listen carefully." The woman took a deep breath. She clasped and unclasped her hands. Her brown eyes glowed, boring into Ginger's until Ginger felt hypnotized and unable to turn away. She waited, hearing the bus approach.

The woman's words came softly. Sweetly. Proudly.

"Ginger," she said, "I am your mother."

Chapter Ten

GINGER'S KNEES SHOOK AS she boarded the bus. She walked to her usual seat beside Karie, holding on to the backs of the other seats to steady herself.

"Are you all right?" Karie asked. "You look pale."

Ginger sat down and looked past Karie, out the window. The woman was walking briskly toward the corner. As the bus passed her, Ginger saw the white car, parked just around the corner.

Karie turned to see what Ginger was watching. "Oh," Karie said. "That's her, isn't it? The woman from your birthday party."

Ginger nodded.

Karie looked closely at Ginger. "Is something wrong?"

"She talked to me."

"What did she say?"

"I'll tell you later," Ginger said. "When we're alone."

It was lunchtime before Ginger and Karie had a chance to talk. They sat in a corner of the school yard, leaning back against the fence, and Ginger told her friend everything that had happened: how the white car waited in the parking lot after school every day, how she called Ginger's home but never left her name, and finally, how the woman came to the bus stop and talked to her.

"Who is she?" Karie asked. "What does she want?"

Even though there was no one near them, Ginger leaned close to Karie and whispered, "She said she's my mother."

"What?" Karie cried. "She must be crazy. Why would she say that?"

"The bus came right after she told me, so I didn't ask any questions."

"Well, we know she's wrong."

"Do we?"

Karie's mouth dropped open, and she frowned at Ginger. "You don't believe her, do you?"

"I don't want to believe her, but I thought about

it all morning. Did you ever notice that everyone in my family, except me, is tall? This woman is short, like I am."

"That doesn't prove anything."

"I'm so different from Mom and Dad, and Laura. They don't care at all about sports. Mom and Laura love fancy parties; I hate getting dressed up. I'm not mechanical like Dad, either."

"Your mom and dad told us about the day you were born," Karie said, "about having the flat tire on their way to the hospital."

"Maybe they made up a convincing story because they don't want me to know I'm adopted."

"Why wouldn't they want you to know? It's an honor to be adopted. If you're adopted, it means your parents really wanted you and didn't just get stuck with you."

Ginger said, "Her hair is reddish brown, like mine. Tipper and Laura both have Mom's dark hair."

"That's true. You don't look like the rest of your family."

"I've always been the one who is different. When we have family votes, it's usually four to one."

"If you think for one second that this woman is telling you the truth," Karie said, "you had better call your parents right now. Tell them what has happened and ask if it's true. If it is, they'll explain, and they'll tell you what to do if she keeps bothering you. If it isn't true, you can tell the woman to bug off."

If it's true, Ginger thought, I'm not sure I want to know. There must be some reason why they hid the truth from me. Maybe there's something terrible in my background. Maybe my father was a murderer.

She did not confide her worries to Karie. She said, "If I called Mom and Dad about this, they would hop on the first plane for home, and I don't want that. Dad looked forward to this conference for months, and Mom's customer needs help with her daughter's wedding. This can wait until they get home."

"When will they be back?" Karie asked.

"Mom arrives Sunday morning; Dad gets home Sunday night."

"That's three days from now," Karie said. "I don't think you should wait three days before you tell someone. Maybe you should tell Mr. Wren, or the school counselor."

Ginger shook her head. "They would call Mom and Dad."

"We could tell my parents," Karie said, "but they would call your mom and dad, too."

"I'm not going to tell anyone but you."

"You can't just pretend this hasn't happened. You have to do something."

"I will as soon as Mom and Dad get home."

"What if she keeps following you and watching you?"

"She's already done that for four days, and it hasn't hurt anything. She was just waiting for a chance to talk to me when there wasn't anyone else around."

"What if she tries to kidnap you?" Karie said. "If she thinks she's your mother, she might want you to go and live with her."

Ginger hadn't thought of that possibility. She shuddered. "She isn't big enough to force me to go with her," Ginger said.

"She could get a gun," Karie said.

Then, seeing the look of horror on Ginger's face, Karie added, "She probably won't do that. She's probably just a nutsy lady who has you mixed up with someone else."

The bell rang, announcing the end of lunch period. Ginger and Karie had no afternoon classes together, so they went separate ways when they got inside the building.

Beth Sumner was in Ginger's first afternoon class. "It doesn't look good for Mr. Wren," Beth said. "My mom called all the parents whose kids are on the basketball team, and a lot of them refused to take sides in the matter. Mom says there are too many parents who have business connections with the Vaughns. One man even said, 'It's a choice of the coach's job or my job, and

I have to look out for my family.' Of the parents who didn't already speak at the first hearing, the only one who agreed to talk in favor of Mr. Wren was Mr. Randolph, Nancy's dad."

"If he does," Ginger said, "he's probably going to lose his biggest client." Unless, Ginger added to herself, I hand over my tapes before Mr. Randolph speaks.

Class started. Ginger tried to concentrate on the history of Mexico, but her mind kept returning to the puzzling encounter at the bus stop. She wondered if she should talk further with the woman. She was certain the woman would be waiting for her in the parking lot. If Ginger wanted to hear more, all she had to do was walk to the woman's car and listen.

In spite of Karie's worry, Ginger did not believe the woman meant to hurt her or force her to do anything that Ginger did not want to do. If she intended to kidnap me, Ginger thought, she would have done it by now.

I want to find out *why* she thinks she's my mother, Ginger thought. Even if the woman is a real nut case, what does it hurt to listen to her story?

And if—just for the sake of argument, Ginger told herself—*if* the woman is telling the truth, then I should ask her for medical information.

The possibility that the woman might really be who she said she was fascinated Ginger in a horrible sort of way. Nothing dramatic had ever happened to Ginger. This was the kind of event that movies were made of. Not that she would ever want such a movie to be made. Even if the woman's story was true, it wouldn't change Ginger's love for Mom and Dad, or for Laura and Tipper.

Still, it would be the most unusual thing that had ever happened to her or to any of her friends.

I won't get in her car, Ginger decided. I'll just stand there in the parking lot, in full view of the kids who are getting on the bus and the parents who always park and wait to pick up their kids, and listen to what she wants to tell me.

That will be perfectly safe. One scream and there would be ten people beside me.

She told Karie what she planned to do.

"I'll come with you," Karie said.

Ginger shook her head. "I need to talk to her alone."

"Then I'll stand by the door and watch," Karie said. "If she threatens you, or does anything to scare you, rub your left ear. That will be the signal for me to get help."

"You're making this sound like a dangerous encounter with a criminal, instead of a simple conversation," Ginger said. "I won't need to rub my left ear." She smiled at Karie. "But I will feel less nervous if I know you are watching us. Thanks."

When school was out, Ginger and Karie hurried to the main door. Ginger looked across the parking area. "There she is," she said. "The white car with the yellow ribbon on the antenna."

"Don't take any chances," Karie said. "If you don't like what she says, give me the signal. And don't talk so long that we miss the bus."

Ginger nodded. Taking a deep breath, she walked toward the car.

"Good luck," Karie said.

As Ginger approached, the woman got out and came to meet her. "Thank you for coming," she said.

"Why did you say that you're my mother?"

"Let's sit in the car to talk."

"No. We'll have to talk here."

The woman nodded.

"Who are you?" Ginger asked. "What's your name?"

"My name is Joyce Enderly. I had a baby girl— you—thirteen years ago, and I was not able to keep you. Your father was killed in a motorcycle accident before you were born. We weren't married, and he never knew I was pregnant. I had no relatives to help me, and no way to support a child. I decided the best thing I could do for you was to let you be adopted by a loving family."

Joyce Enderly brushed a tear from her cheek. "I released you to an adoption agency, and agreed that I would have no further contact with you. I wasn't told the names of your adoptive parents. I tried to forget about you and start a new life, but I always wondered how you were and what you looked like. Every year on your birthday, I would go out to eat, to celebrate."

"And this year you saw me in the restaurant."

"That's right. I saw you come in and was struck by how much you look like me. I told myself I was imagining things. But then the waiter announced it was your birthday. And I knew. I knew right then who you are."

"Lots of babies are born on the same day every year," Ginger said. "That doesn't prove anything."

"I looked at the people you were with, and I saw that you look much more like me than you look like them. Your brother and sister resemble their mother. But you look like me."

"Mom says I look like my grandmother did, when she was my age."

"Then they never told you that you're adopted?"

"No."

"I had hoped they would tell you the truth, right from the start. When I told you that I'm your mother, I thought you would know instantly that it was true. I even imagined that you had been hoping to find me someday."

"My parents told me about the day I was born. I

came two weeks early, and they had a flat tire on their way to the hospital."

Joyce's eyes flashed angrily. "They are lying," she said.

Ginger took a step back.

"They were not present when you were born. I was. Me! Only me, and the doctor. You were born at Swedish Hospital."

Ginger shook her head no. "I was born in Texas," she said. "My family lived in Houston then."

"No!" Joyce clenched and unclenched her fists, as if she wanted to strike something—or someone. "They're lying about that, too. You were born in Seattle."

This woman is weird, Ginger thought. When we started talking, she smiled at me the way Grandma and Grandpa do, all loving and kind, as if I could never possibly do anything wrong. Now she looks furious, as if I am responsible for whatever is wrong in her life.

"Go home and look in the mirror," Joyce said. "Then you'll know who is lying and who is telling the truth. You have lived with them, but you are *my* flesh and blood."

The school buses started their engines. Karie walked partway to the bus and stopped, watching Ginger.

"I have to go now," Ginger said, "or I'll miss my bus."

95

"I can drive you home."

"No, thanks. I'm supposed to take the bus."

"I'll wait here for you tomorrow," Joyce said. "Same time."

"Are you coming?" Karie called.

Ginger hurried away from the woman, toward the bus.

"Look in the mirror!" Joyce shouted after her. "You'll see the proof!"

Ginger and Karie boarded the bus a second before the door closed. "What did she say?" Karie asked as the bus pulled away.

Ginger felt the way she had the day she accidentally swallowed a whole ice cube. There was a cold hard lump in the middle of her chest. But this lump didn't melt, the way the ice cube had.

When she thought about what the woman had said, the lump got bigger. And colder.

Chapter Eleven

JOYCE ENDERLY DIALED THE number from memory, even though it had been three years since she had spoken to her brother-in-law. Arnie's brother would help her; she was sure of it. Jake, like Arnie, would do anything for money.

"Hello?"

"Hi, Jake. It's me. Joyce."

"Forget it. Whatever it is you want, forget it."

"I can pay."

"How much?"

"Three thousand."

"Yeah? What did you do, rob that mental hospital you were in?"

"I left there a year ago and I'm not going back. I'm cured."

"That'll be the day."

"Do you want the job or don't you?"

"Where are you?"

"In Seattle, same as you."

"What do I have to do?"

"Help me arrange a meeting with a thirteen-year-old girl."

"My brother's in prison for doing that."

"Four thousand. Cash."

"You got a deal."

Karie went home with Ginger. "Do you have family photo albums?" she asked.

"We have some scrapbooks."

"Let's look in them. Go back to the year you were born and see what we find."

"I'm not sure where they are."

"What about a birth certificate? You must have a birth certificate somewhere."

"Let's look in Mom's office."

The girls read the labels on every file folder in Mrs. Shaw's file cabinet. The labels said things like ANDERSON WEDDING or MICROCHIP EMPLOYEE PICNIC. None of the files held personal information.

Next they went into Mr. and Mrs. Shaw's bedroom and looked on the closet shelf. They found only clothing and a stack of old magazines about player pianos.

"The family room," Ginger said. "Let's try that cupboard above the one where we keep games."

The cupboard revealed a stack of scrapbooks. Ginger flipped through them until she came to the year she was born. She found a picture of her mom, looking very pregnant and reading a book to little Laura. And she found a birth announcement, giving the date and time Ginger was born. It said she weighed five pounds, twelve ounces.

A brief clipping from a Texas newspaper titled "Births" listed *Shaw, Duane and Margaret; girl, Ginger Marie; Sagebrush Hospital.*

There was a picture of Mrs. Shaw in a hospital bed, holding a newborn baby, and a picture of Grandma holding the baby while Laura mugged at the camera.

"I never noticed before," Ginger said, "but I do look a lot like Grandma did before her hair turned gray."

"You are definitely not adopted," Karie said.

"No." Ginger smiled. "No, I'm not. I didn't really believe I was, but Joyce was so insistent that I let my imagination get carried away."

"I'm glad that storm has blown over," Karie said as they put the scrapbooks away.

"I won't talk to Joyce again," Ginger said. "I probably should not have talked to her at all, but she took me by surprise this morning at the bus stop, and then I got curious and so I wanted to know more."

The phone rang. Nancy Randolph told Ginger, "I'm resigning as student council president. Effective immediately."

"Why?" Ginger said. "What's wrong?" She motioned for Karie to pick up the kitchen phone and listen.

Nancy said, "My dad is practicing a speech for tomorrow night; he's going to tell the school board they should keep Mr. Wren as coach. If he gives that speech, he'll lose his biggest client—and maybe his job. Dad is doing it to support me, and I can't let him. I'm sorry. I'm going to quit and let someone else represent the council at the meeting. That way, I won't have to go at all, and Dad won't feel that he's letting me down by not speaking in favor of Mr. Wren."

"You don't have to resign," Ginger said. "If you stay home from tomorrow's meeting, everyone will understand."

"If I can't do the job right," Nancy said, "I want to let someone else do it. Will you come to a quick meeting during lunch tomorrow? Just long enough to elect a new president?"

Ginger and Karie agreed to attend the meeting.

After Nancy's call, Ginger said, "Nancy shouldn't have to quit as president because of Mrs. Vaughn."

"I can't believe how many people took Mrs. Vaughn's side," Karie said. "Some of them have never even been to one of the games, but now they act as if Mr. Wren has ruined their kids' future. I wish we could prove what a good coach Mr. Wren is."

I can, Ginger thought. That's the problem.

Mrs. Shaw called just after Karie left.

"Everything is fine," Ginger assured her mother. "Karie came over, and we looked at some of the old scrapbooks. We found my baby pictures."

"Weren't you the cutest baby ever?" Mrs. Shaw said.

"You know what I used to think, when I was little?" Ginger said. "I used to think I was adopted."

"Whatever made you think that?" her mother asked.

"Because I was short and the rest of you are tall. And because of my reddish hair."

"Why didn't you ask me?" Her mother sounded indignant, and even without seeing her, Ginger knew that Mrs. Shaw had one fist on her hip. "You know I would have told you the truth."

"I thought there was some deep, dark secret in my background."

Mrs. Shaw laughed. "It seems to me Laura went through that, too," she said. "Maybe all kids imagine they're adopted."

"Laura talked to Marcus's mother this morning," Ginger said. "She said Tipper and Marcus were getting along great."

"I called Tipper," Mrs. Shaw said. "He burped for me."

"Lucky you."

"What happened at the school board meeting?" Mrs. Shaw asked.

"A lot of people testified against Mr. Wren."

"I was afraid of that. Victoria Vaughn will pressure everyone she can. A mob mentality takes over in situations like this. People take sides and get too angry."

"The final hearing is tomorrow. Mr. Randolph is planning to speak in favor of keeping Mr. Wren, and Nancy's afraid he'll lose his job. It's a mess."

"I know George Randolph," Mrs. Shaw said, "and he'll do what's right, regardless of the consequences. For some people, honor is more important than money, and you know what? I admire that."

They talked a few minutes longer. "I'd better hang up," Mrs. Shaw said, "before we own the telephone company."

"I'll see you Sunday," Ginger said.

"Love you."

"Love you, too."

After Ginger hung up the phone her mother's words replayed in her mind: "For some people, honor is more important than money, and you know what? I admire that."

Do you, Mom? Ginger thought. Would you admire me if I turn my tapes in to the school board and prove that Mr. Wren knows how to coach? Would you admire me if I make Mrs. Vaughn so furious that she never hires you or Laura again?

It's easy to respect someone else for doing what he believes is right even though it risks his income, Ginger thought. But it isn't so easy to risk my own family's income.

As she climbed into bed that night, Ginger looked at her new poster. LIVE WITH PURPOSE AND HONOR.

What is the honorable thing to do? she wondered. I feel loyal to Mr. Wren. But I am *more* loyal to Mom and Laura.

Chapter Twelve

FRIDAY MORNING GINGER AWOKE with a head-ache, still undecided whether or not to turn her tapes over to the school board.

"I have a chemistry lab from four to six," Laura told her, "so I won't be home until almost seven."

"I'm going to the school board hearing tonight," Ginger said. "It starts at six."

"Do you need a ride?"

"Karie's dad is going. He'll pick me up."

"I wonder if Mrs. Vaughn's behind-the-scenes lob-bying will work."

"I hope not. Mr. Wren is a good coach, and we both know what sort of person the Queen is."

"Still, a lot of people will knuckle under and do what Mrs. Vaughn wants rather than lose her business."

Including me? Ginger wondered. Is that what I'm going to do?

Ginger decided not to go home after school, since Laura would not be there. Even though she was convinced that Joyce Enderly had the wrong person, Ginger was uneasy about the possibility of being alone with Joyce again. The woman was so intense, and so positive that she was right. And her mood changes were too rapid and unpredictable.

Ginger would stay at school, watch basketball practice, and then go straight to the hearing in the administration building, directly across the street from the school. She took an extra sandwich and some grapes in her backpack, to have for dinner.

She also took the bag of tapes. Maybe she could turn them in anonymously. She could go to the hearing room early and leave the bag where the school board would see it. She could put a note on it: *Attention! Watch these tapes before you fire Coach Wren.*

Yes, Ginger thought. If I do that, I can help Mr. Wren without hurting Mom and Laura. She was certain that Mrs. Vaughn would not recognize her voice on the tapes. The few times she had helped Laura at Mrs. Vaughn's house, Laura had done the talking.

The only problem would be getting into the hearing room without being seen.

When it was time to leave for school, Ginger watched out the window for a few minutes, hoping to walk to the bus with her neighbor, Eric Konen. Eric did not appear.

He must be sick, Ginger thought. He didn't go to school yesterday, either.

When she could wait no longer, she ran down the sidewalk and around the corner to where she caught the bus.

Joyce Enderly was waiting for her. This time Joyce's car was parked right across from the bus stop, and when Ginger rounded the corner, Joyce came to greet her.

"You're mistaken about who I am," Ginger told her. "I'm not adopted. I found the notice of my birth in the Houston newspaper, and I saw pictures of my mom holding me in the hospital, the day I was born."

"Here is your *real* baby picture," Joyce said. "It's all I've had for thirteen years, until I found you." She held out a faded snapshot, wrinkled from years of handling.

Ginger looked at the picture but did not take it. "It's a pretty baby," she said, "but it isn't me." She saw the school bus approaching.

"I need more time with you," Joyce said. "We can't

keep talking in snatches, always distracted by the bus. Meet me after school today."

"I'm busy after school."

The bus chugged closer.

"Tonight then. At the library."

"No," Ginger said. "I'm sorry to disappoint you, but I am not who you think I am, and I don't want to talk to you anymore."

The bus stopped beside them.

Joyce put her hand on Ginger's arm. She spoke decisively, emphasizing each word: "I am your mother."

Ginger pulled her arm away.

"I'm asking for only a few hours alone with you. To take some pictures, to get to know you better and let you know me."

"You have the wrong person," Ginger said. "I'm not your daughter, and I will not talk to you again. Period."

The door of the bus opened.

Ginger boarded the bus and took her usual place beside Karie.

As the doors moaned shut, Joyce muttered, "Jake will help me. Jake will make you go with me."

Ginger did not hear her.

When Ginger looked out the window, Joyce stared back at her. Tears trickled down Joyce's cheeks. The look on her face was a strange mixture of love and hate.

Ginger shivered and turned away.

The bus moved on.

"She was at the bus stop when I got there," Ginger told Karie. "She still claims she's my mother. She showed me a picture of a newborn baby that she says is me."

"Weird," said Karie. "Did you tell her to quit bugging you?"

"Yes, and I think she finally got the message."

"Good."

"She makes me nervous but I feel sorry for her, too. I think she's mentally unbalanced, or else she wants so much to believe she's found her long-lost daughter that she refuses to accept the truth. Either way, I'll be glad when Mom and Dad get home."

"Did you see the Channel Seven news this morning?" Karie asked.

"No."

"They interviewed Mr. Wren, and then they interviewed Mrs. Vaughn. She claimed he has never taught his players anything about basketball."

"That's not true!"

"I'm only repeating what she said." Karie popped a breath mint into her mouth.

Ginger considered telling Karie her plan to leave the tapes and the note in the hearing room, but she decided it would be best not to tell anyone. Let the tapes be truly anonymous so that Mrs. Vaughn could never discover who to blame.

The lunch hour student council meeting was short. The members refused to let Nancy resign and agreed that she did not have to attend the hearing.

After school, Ginger did her homework in the library. Then she went to the gym, to watch basketball practice.

Mrs. Wren and Dana sat partway up the bleachers. Ginger climbed up and sat beside them.

"Hi, Ginger," Dana said. She busily colored a pony in a coloring book; so far, she'd done a red head and three blue legs. "We're watching Daddy coach."

Mrs. Wren said, "I was restless at home."

"We might have to move," Dana said.

"Mr. Wren isn't going to change schools, is he?" Ginger asked.

"That depends on what happens at the hearing tonight," Mrs. Wren said. "If the board fires him as coach, Bill will apply for a teaching job in a different district. Mountain View Middle School needs a social studies teacher."

"Nobody has questioned his teaching ability," Ginger said. "He's the best teacher we have."

"The school board, and the community, should support him in this situation. Bill can handle Mrs. Vaughn's accusations; she has disliked him ever since she lost the city council election. Every coach—every teacher, for that matter—has to deal with an unreasonable parent once in a while. But when so many others spoke against him . . ." Tears filled Mrs. Wren's eyes, and she had to pause to get control of her voice. "When others spoke against him, it hurt. Were you at the first hearing?"

"Yes."

"Then you know what I'm talking about."

"I don't want to move," Dana said.

"We love our little house," Mrs. Wren said, "and I want the same doctor who delivered Dana to deliver our new baby."

"Mommy!" Dana looked shocked. "You said that's a secret. You said I wasn't supposed to tell anyone, not even Ginger."

"You already told Ginger, remember?"

"Oh." Dana began coloring a green tail on the pony.

"Most of the players' parents have never been to a practice," Mrs. Wren said. "Many have never been to a game. How can they criticize the way Bill coaches?"

"The other parents were pressured by Mrs. Vaughn," Ginger said. "Just about everyone in town does business with Vaughn Enterprises; people were protecting their jobs when they agreed with her."

"I know. Several people told us about her tactics."

"Not all of the parents spoke at the hearing," Ginger said.

"If you don't speak out against something that is wrong," Mrs. Wren said, "you imply by your silence that it's right. Even those who didn't speak at all let him down."

Like me, Ginger thought. She remembered one evening a few weeks earlier when Tipper had come to the dinner table puffed up with pride.

"A kid in my class told a nasty joke at lunch," Tipper said. "Everyone laughed, except me."

Tipper smiled at his parents, clearly expecting them to praise him.

Instead, Mr. Shaw had asked, "Did you speak up? Did you tell your friends that such jokes are not funny?"

Tipper admitted he had said nothing.

"Then you might as well have laughed," Mr. Shaw said. "By keeping still, you implied it's okay to tell nasty jokes."

"I didn't want to make my friends mad at me," Tipper said.

"You missed a chance to stand up for what's right," Mrs. Shaw added. "People who are offended by the truth aren't very good friends anyway."

Dana dropped a crayon, and Mrs. Wren grabbed it before it could roll through the opening in the bleachers.

I'm missing a chance, too, Ginger thought, but there's a lot more to lose than the friendship of some giggling first graders.

"I'm hungry," Dana said. "Let's go to McDonald's."

"Not tonight," Mrs. Wren said.

"I want french fries," Dana said.

Ginger opened her lunch sack and offered Dana a cluster of grapes.

"Thanks," Dana said. "You're my pal." She popped a grape in her mouth.

"If Bill is let go in the middle of a season," Mrs. Wren said, "he'll never get another coaching job. Potential employers wouldn't know about Mrs. Vaughn's meddling; they would know only that Bill got fired." She wiped her eyes with a tissue. Then she blew her nose, and sat up straight. "I didn't mean to dump our problems on you," she said. "Just ignore me; I get weepy when I'm pregnant."

"Daddy says he has lots of friends," Dana said, "and maybe they'll make it so we don't have to move."

"You talk too much," Mrs. Wren said. Then she laughed and added, "I can't imagine where she gets it."

Dana swallowed the last grape and handed the stem to her mother. "I'm still hungry," she said.

Ginger reached for her lunch sack, but Mrs. Wren stopped her.

"No more grapes," she said. "Put your crayons in the box, Dana; it's almost five o'clock—time to go home and start dinner."

"What are we having?" Dana asked.

"Macaroni and cheese. Again."

"I LOVE macaroni and cheese," Dana said. "Almost as much as red jelly beans."

"Good luck tonight," Ginger said as Mrs. Wren and Dana started down the aisle.

"Thanks. We'll need it."

Ginger watched a little more of the practice, but she couldn't concentrate. She decided to go over to the administration building, even though the hearing wasn't until six. Maybe the room would be unlocked. Maybe she could go in and leave the tapes and be done with it.

She retrieved the bag of tapes from her locker. The anonymous note, which she had written during study period, was already taped to the bag. She carried the bag down the hall toward the front door.

Partway to the door, she stopped. I am a coward, she thought, to do this anonymously. An unsigned note might not be taken seriously. The board members might think it's a student prank. What if they ignore the bag of videotapes until after the meeting? Then it would be too late for the tapes to help.

The board would not be able to ignore a person. If I

stand in front of them and hand them the tapes, and say the tapes are proof that Mr. Wren is a good coach, they'll have to pay attention.

Ginger imagined Mrs. Vaughn's furious reaction when she saw what the tapes contained. She also imagined Mr. Wren's reaction. And Mrs. Wren's.

What would Mom say? And Laura?

Live with Purpose and Honor.

I can't just sneak into the hearing room, leave the tapes, and hope the board watches them, Ginger decided. I have to make it happen. I need to stand up at the meeting and explain what I have. It is the honorable thing to do, and Mom and Laura will understand. I hope.

She pulled the anonymous note from the bag, crumpled it, and threw it in a trash container.

If Mrs. Vaughn withdraws her business from Celebrations and from B.A. Catering, Ginger thought, I'll do more baby-sitting, and use the money to help with Laura's tuition. I'll baby-sit every night, if I have to. And when Laura does get catering jobs, I'll go along and help her for free.

Filled with determination, Ginger headed out the door. She wanted to be first to sign up to speak at the hearing. If she went first, it might save a lot of trouble for other people, like Mr. Randolph.

The board might not play all the tapes at the hearing, but if they played enough to see that Mrs. Vaughn was wrong, they would probably cancel the rest of tonight's hearing. They might vote to drop the whole matter. Mr. Randolph would never have to give his speech, and neither would anyone else whom Mrs. Vaughn had pressured. I might be saving Mr. Randolph's job, as well as Mr. Wren's, Ginger thought.

For the first time since her birthday, Ginger did not look at the parking lot before she left the building. For the first time since her birthday, the white car—and the woman who drove it—were not uppermost in her mind as she stepped outside.

The activity bus had not arrived yet, and the regular after-school buses had long since departed. Rain darkened the concrete, spattering on Ginger's shoulders. Chilled, she pulled the hood of her sweatshirt up over her hair, blocking her side vision.

The parking area was empty, except for one car waiting in the shadows beyond the streetlight. The wet yellow ribbon dangling from its antenna waved gently in the breeze.

Ginger did not notice. Her eyes, and her thoughts, were focused on the administration building across the street.

She crossed the parking lot, head down because of the rain, and hurried toward the street, clutching the bag of tapes.

Chapter Thirteen

"WAIT!"

Ginger recognized Joyce's voice immediately. She glanced over her shoulder, surprised that she had not noticed the white car.

Joyce stood beside the car, waving at Ginger.

Ginger kept walking. She had told Joyce she would not talk to her anymore, and she intended to keep that promise.

"Ginger!" The voice was louder now. "Wait! I need to talk to you."

Ginger broke into a run, rushing toward the administration building. She heard footsteps on the pavement behind her, but she did not look back.

A man's voice sliced through the rain. "We have your little brother," he said.

Ginger froze, horrified.

"I suggest you stop and talk to us," the man said.

Slowly, Ginger turned around.

"That's better." The man wore jeans and a dark jacket; his hair was covered by a baseball cap. He spoke with a slight southern drawl, as calmly as if he were asking her to please pass the cupcakes. "Now, don't even think about yelling for help, little lady," he said. "Because if you do, we won't be able to take your brother home again."

"Who are you?" Ginger asked.

"It doesn't matter who I am. What's important is who *you* are."

"I'm not who she thinks I am," Ginger said, pointing at Joyce, who stood beside the man.

"It seems you're a bit mixed up about that," the man said. "My friend needs to spend some time with you, and she tells me you haven't been very polite."

"Where is Tipper?" Ginger said.

"You'll get to see him," the man said, "as soon as you do what Joyce wants."

"How do I know you have my brother?" Ginger said. "Maybe you're bluffing."

"Oh, we have him all right," the man replied. "He's at Joyce's apartment, waiting for you. All you have to do is get in the car and let us drive you over there. Then, after you've had your picture taken, and had a nice little mother/daughter chat with Joyce, we'll untie your brother and take both of you home."

Ginger's mind raced, trying to think what to do. She found it hard to believe that they could have kidnapped Tipper. He and Marcus stuck together as if their clothes were glued, and Marcus's mom would be especially vigilant about watching them this week, when she had full responsibility for both boys.

If Ginger got in the car and went with Joyce and the man, she had no way to control where they would take her. They might not go to Joyce's apartment. They might take her a thousand miles away and make her pretend to be Joyce's daughter. She might never see Tipper, or the rest of her family, again.

But what if the man spoke the truth? What if he and Joyce had tricked Tipper into going with them? What if Tipper really was locked in an apartment somewhere nearby, and the only hope of rescuing him was for Ginger to go along with what Joyce wanted?

If I go with them, Ginger thought, no one will know I've gone. No one will know where I am. I won't be missed until after six o'clock, when Karie realizes I'm not at the school board meeting. And she'll wait until after the meeting to call and ask Laura why I wasn't there. By then, it will be too late to help me.

The rain came harder, drenching Ginger's sweat-shirt. An icy fear soaked into every pore of her body.

I need to buy some time, Ginger thought. I need to stay here until other people arrive. Then I'll signal for help somehow.

She realized the man was waiting for her response.

"Why do I have to get my picture taken?" she asked.

"The only picture I have of you is the one taken when you were newborn," Joyce said. "A mother needs to have current pictures of her daughter."

Ginger wanted to shout, *I am not your daughter!*, but she swallowed the words. There was nothing to be gained by making Joyce and the man angry.

"I'll go home with you," she said. "But I can't go until after I speak at the school board meeting."

The man's eyes closed slightly. "You're stalling," he said. "You can come with us now."

Ginger held up the bag of tapes. "There's a special hearing tonight," she said, "and this is crucial evidence. If I don't show up, my favorite teacher is going to get fired as coach of the girls' basketball team."

"So, let him get fired," the man said. "Who cares?"

"I care," Ginger said. "Lots of people care."

"We don't," the man said.

"We could wait inside," Ginger said. "There's a lobby area next to the room where the school board meets. We can sit there and get better acquainted." She looked directly at Joyce and added, "The coach's wife is expecting a baby. If he gets fired, they won't have enough money."

"What time is the hearing?" Joyce asked.

"Six o'clock."

"That's almost an hour from now." The man put a hand on Joyce's arm. "If we leave right now, no one sees us. If we wait until the meeting has started, a lot of people will be here. That isn't good."

Ginger noticed that neither Joyce nor the man mentioned that an hour was too long to leave Tipper alone in Joyce's apartment. I don't think he's really there, she thought. I think they made that up, to get me to go with them.

"If anyone wonders who you are," Ginger said, "I'll just say you're relatives." She forced herself to smile at Joyce. "That would be the truth, wouldn't it, Mother?"

"Oooh," Joyce said. "Oh, my darling, I've waited so long to hear you call me that."

The smile stayed on Ginger's face, but she felt as if she were wearing a mask. The real Ginger was not smiling.

Inside, she was boiling with rage at this couple. How dare they try to force her to go with them? How dare they bring Tipper into it? Even if they were lying about Tipper's whereabouts, even if he was at Marcus's house right now, happily burping or playing Batman, it made her furious that they would use her love for her brother to scare her into going with them.

As the fury bubbled inside her, her determination grew. She would not go meekly with Joyce and her accomplice, now or later. She would try to outsmart them.

"It's really important for me to be at the meeting," Ginger said. "I'm the only one who can prove that Mr. Wren is a good coach, and if I don't speak tonight, he'll get fired."

The man reached for Ginger's bag, opened it, and looked inside.

"If your evidence is these videos," he said, "you can leave them here, and let someone else present them."

"The school board members won't watch the videos in time if I'm not here to explain what they are." Still smiling, she took a step closer to Joyce. "I think you will be proud of me when I speak to the school board, Mother," she said. She looked into Joyce's eyes and saw again the strange, hypnotic glow.

"Yes," Joyce said. "I will be proud."

"If we're going to take this kid to your apartment," the man said, "let's do it. Waiting around here for some meeting is crazy."

"We don't have to stay for the whole meeting," Ginger said. "I'll sign up to be the first speaker, and as soon as I have my turn, we'll leave."

"And you'll go home with me?" Joyce said. "We'll take some pictures and have a good talk?"

"We can start talking right now," Ginger said. "Let's go in, Mother, out of the rain." She reached for Joyce's hand.

Joyce clasped Ginger's fingers and climbed the steps with her.

Behind them, the man said, "Don't blame me if this doesn't work out."

Ginger opened the door, and she and Joyce walked in, with the man at their heels. They sat on a wooden bench in the lobby area outside the hearing room.

"When people start coming," the man said, "I'll be watching you. If you say or do anything to try to get out of going with us, you'll regret it. And so will your little brother."

Ginger ignored the man and spoke to Joyce. "Tell me about yourself," she said. "I want to know everything about you. Where you live, what kind of work you do, what your hobbies are. Start with the week I was born, and tell me everything."

Joyce began to talk, and Ginger tried to act as if she were listening. In reality, she was trying to think of ways to signal for help without having Joyce and the man catch on.

Perhaps when she wrote her name on the sign-up sheet to speak at the meeting, she could add the word *help*. But the next person to sign in would probably say something, maybe even ask who needs help, and then Joyce and the man would know what she had done.

If only she could be sure whether they really had Tipper or not. If they didn't, she could simply wait until several people had arrived and then speak up. But what if she did that and it turned out Tipper was being held hostage somewhere? The man would run, and Joyce, too. They could get away and get to Tipper before the police could find them.

I should have written down the license number of Joyce's car, Ginger realized. *I had plenty of chances to do so; why didn't I ever think about it?*

A school-district employee arrived. Ginger recognized her from the previous hearing, when the woman had sat at the table with the school board members, apparently taking minutes on a notebook computer. The secretary unlocked the hearing room, brought out the notices with instructions for signing up to speak, and laid the sign-up sheet and pencil on the table. Then she went into the hearing room.

"Excuse me," Ginger told Joyce, who was talking

about her job. "I need to sign up, so I'll be the first speaker."

She walked to the table and put her name down at the top of the page. As she wrote, the man stood beside her, looking over her shoulder. She realized he was watching to see if she wrote a message in addition to her name.

When Ginger sat back down, the man stood next to the door. Every time she looked at him, his eyes were on her, watching her every move. He's ready to run, if need be, Ginger thought. If I yelled Help! right now, he would be in the car before anyone could get here to see what was wrong.

She wondered where he would go. Would he drive to Joyce's apartment and untie Tipper and . . .

Ginger refused to let her imagination travel that road.

She would have to be careful, to protect Tipper. Whatever move she made, it must be something that the man did not recognize as a plea for help.

While Joyce talked on, Ginger looked carefully at her and at the man. She noticed exactly what they were wearing. She estimated how tall they were, and how old. She paid attention to the Fred's Fish House logo on the man's baseball cap. If she got away from them, she would be able to give the police an accurate description.

No, she told herself. Not *if* I get away; *when* I get away.

A group of five other people arrived. Mrs. Sumner signed her name below Ginger's before the group went into the hearing room.

Joyce talked on about her life, seemingly unaware of what was going on around her. She told of getting married, a year after Ginger's birth. "I wanted another baby," Joyce said, "but it never happened, and two years later the doctors told me I would never have another child. That's when I made up my mind to find you."

"Why didn't you adopt a child?" Ginger asked.

"No! I wanted you. Only you." Joyce took Ginger's hand and held it. Ginger wanted to pull her hand away, but she gritted her teeth and did nothing.

"My first husband didn't understand," Joyce said. "He thought I was a fanatic. He divorced me after I found you the first time. You were three then, and such a pretty little girl. But my husband sent me to a hospital and the doctors lied to me. My second husband, Arnie, agreed to help me get you back. We found you again when you were ten. We were in Montana on vacation, but we had a small problem. . . ." She stopped talking in midsentence, dropped Ginger's hand, and fidgeted nervously with the hem of her sweater. "You know about that," she mumbled.

"No," Ginger said as she tried to make sense of Joyce's rambling. "What kind of a problem?"

Joyce did not reply for over a minute. Then she said, "This time, Jake is helping me. For four thousand dollars."

"You *paid* him to kidnap Tipper?" Ginger said.

"I paid him to arrange our meeting. How he did it was up to him."

"Is he armed?" Ginger asked.

"I don't know. Probably. He's done this sort of thing before. He even gave me a secret code word to use, in case something seemed wrong and I wanted to call the deal off. Why would I call it off, after I paid him in advance?"

As soon as Joyce said "secret code word," Ginger knew how she could signal for help. When Karie arrived, Ginger would rub her left ear. That signal had been Karie's suggestion, the day she watched Ginger talk to Joyce in front of the school. She was pretty sure Karie would catch on, especially when she saw Joyce.

More people arrived. A group of Ginger's classmates came in, said "hi" to Ginger, and then, seeing that Ginger was talking to the woman, waved and went on into the room. Nancy Randolph and her dad came; Mr. Randolph signed the speakers' list.

Mr. and Mrs. Wren came in, holding hands and

looking solemn. They went straight to the front, where chairs had been reserved for them.

The lobby area grew crowded. Four people lined up to add their names to the list of speakers. A photographer from the *Daily Journal*, laden with camera bags, made his way to the front of the room.

Mrs. Vaughn arrived, smiling and acting as if this were one of her parties. Ginger noticed that Polly was not with her. Neither was Mr. Vaughn. Come to think of it, Mr. Vaughn had not been at the other meeting, either. Maybe he was out of town. Or maybe he didn't approve of his wife's activities.

Where was Karie? Karie was the only one who would understand the signal. What if Karie's plans had changed? What if she didn't come to the meeting?

Chapter
Fourteen

GINGER GLANCED AT HER watch. Three minutes to six. The meeting room was nearly full. Ginger scanned the rows of people, wondering if she had somehow missed Karie.

"It's almost time for the hearing to begin," Ginger said. "I have to go in the room, so I'm ready when they call my name."

"Don't try anything funny," the man said. "I'm watching you."

Ginger found a seat near the back. Joyce sat beside her, but the man remained standing, just inside the door.

Karie did not come.

The school board members entered through a side door at the front of the room and sat at a long table, facing the audience. The secretary came in and sat at the end of the table. She typed something into her computer.

Mr. Hixler called the meeting to order, and the buzz of conversation ceased.

Mrs. Vaughn sat on the center aisle, right next to the microphone. Ginger knew from last time that this was where members of the audience stood to make their remarks.

Ginger's head ached. She had too many problems all overlapping at one time. It would be hard enough to stand beside Mrs. Vaughn and offer proof that Mr. Wren coached his team well. But to do it while Joyce and the man watched and waited for her, and to know that Tipper might be in danger, was almost more than she could stand.

And what if Karie didn't come? How could she signal for help? For all she knew, the man concealed a gun under his jacket. She had heard of cases where someone fired shots in a crowded room; she didn't want that to happen here.

Mr. Hixler read the petition to remove Mr. Wren and then said, "A large number of people have signed up to speak tonight. You are each limited to three minutes. If, when it is your turn to talk, you feel that previous speakers have already made the points you wanted to make, please relinquish your time so that the hearing is not unnecessarily long. Are there any questions?"

No one spoke.

"I call the first speaker: Ginger Shaw."

Ginger walked to the microphone, her heart hammering. Mrs. Vaughn smiled warmly at her, clearly expecting that Ginger was about to speak in favor of firing Mr. Wren.

Ginger returned Mrs. Vaughn's smile. You think I'm a wimp who's going to do what you want just because you hire my sister, Ginger thought. Well, guess again. I'm not who *you* think I am, either. I live with purpose and honor. Starting now.

"I want to be a sports announcer," Ginger said, "so I go to a lot of the girls' basketball practices. I videotape them and make up play-by-play descriptions, as if I were broadcasting a game."

She took the three videotapes out of the bag. "These are tapes of some of the practices. They show Mr. Wren instructing the players, and teaching them drills, and leading conditioning exercises, and showing them how to shoot."

A murmur rippled through the room. Beside her, Ginger heard Mrs. Vaughn say, "What?"

"I hope you will play my videos before you continue with this hearing," Ginger said. "They prove that Mr. Wren *is* a good coach, and the players learn a lot from him."

"Please bring the videos forward," Mr. Hixler said.

As Ginger walked to the front of the room, some of the students began to applaud. The man from the *Daily Journal* jumped up and snapped Ginger's picture as she handed over the tapes.

Mr. Hixler banged his gavel. "Order, please," he said. The kids quit clapping, but low voices continued to whisper while Mr. Hixler conferred briefly with the rest of the board members.

Ginger looked back at the audience. Nancy Randolph gave her the thumbs-up sign; Mrs. Vaughn glared angrily. Mrs. Wren mouthed the words *thank you*.

At the rear of the room, Joyce beamed. The man with Joyce stared.

Karie rushed into the room. The back of Ginger's scalp prickled with excitement.

Ginger watched Karie look around the audience. She waited until Karie saw her at the front of the room. Then, when she was certain Karie was looking at her, she put her hand on her left ear and rubbed it.

Her eyes locked with Karie's across the crowd. She saw Karie frown. Please understand, Ginger thought. Please, please get my message.

Karie kept looking at Ginger.

Ginger fiddled with the collar of her sweatshirt and then quickly rubbed her ear again.

She saw Karie look both ways. Nervous sweat trickled down the back of Ginger's neck. She was sure Karie would recognize Joyce. She hoped Karie would not say anything to her, or do anything obvious. Karie had no way of knowing that Joyce was not alone.

Ginger saw Karie notice Joyce.

Mr. Hixler said, "We will watch one of these video-tapes now, before we proceed to the next speaker."

"Thank you," Ginger said.

Karie left.

Two board members rolled a large television set on a stand from behind the table. A VCR was on a shelf beneath the TV. The school board members left their seats and stood at the side of the room, where they could see the screen. Rather than returning to the back of the room, Ginger stood with them.

The crowd quieted as the secretary inserted Ginger's tape.

Mrs. Vaughn stood and spoke into the microphone.

"The first speaker's three minutes are up. It's time for the second speaker."

"Because of the unusual nature of Ginger Shaw's testimony," Mr. Hixler said, "I am granting her additional time. Could someone please turn the lights down?"

The lights dimmed. People who were seated in the back rows stood to get a better view of the screen.

Ginger's video began. When she had rewound the tapes, she had been careful to stop each of them in a spot where Mr. Wren was giving instructions. This video began with him showing the players how to do man-to-man defense.

"Turn up the volume," someone called.

Mr. Hixler clicked a button on the remote control.

Mr. Wren's voice filled the hearing room—teaching the girls and encouraging them when they made mistakes. One section showed the players doing a layup drill where the players were in two lines, half on the left of the basket and half on the right. The first player in the right line tried to make a layup shot; the lead player on the left got the rebound and passed the ball to the next player on the right. As soon as each player had a turn, she went to the end of the opposite line. The lines kept running toward the basket, with the lead players shooting and rebounding as fast as they could while Mr. Wren clapped and cheered them on. When a player missed, Mr. Wren suggested a better way to try it next time. The room was quiet as everyone watched the television screen.

Everyone except the man in the Fred's Fish House baseball cap, who still stood in the rear doorway. Even in the dim light, Ginger could see that he continued to watch her.

Hurry, Karie, she thought. I can't stay up here in front forever. When they stop the video, I'll have to return to the back of the room. He and Joyce will expect me to leave with them, and if I don't . . .

The video was still playing when a cellular telephone, which sat next to the secretary's computer, rang. She picked it up, talked briefly, and hung up. She wrote something on a piece of paper and took the paper to Mr. Hixler.

He read what she had written. Then he stopped the video. "Lights up, please," he said.

When the room was bright again Mr. Hixler said, "We're going to take a two-minute break so that I can ask this speaker a few questions about her tapes. Please stay in your seats. The hearing will resume in two minutes."

He handed the piece of paper to one of the other board members as he motioned for Ginger to follow him. She did.

He led her out the side door at the front of the room.

Karie and two police officers waited in the hall.

"You *were* signaling for help, weren't you?" Karie asked.

"Yes!" Ginger quickly explained what had happened. "They might be lying about Tipper," she added, "but I'm not sure."

"No one has reported a missing boy," Officer Hayworth said.

Ginger told the police Marcus's last name and where he lived, so they could check to see if Tipper was there. They radioed for additional police to come to the administration building.

She described Joyce's car and told where it was parked. She wished again she had thought to get the license plate number.

"Are they armed?" Officer Tyle asked.

"Joyce isn't," Ginger said. "I don't know about him."

"Mr. Hixler," Officer Hayworth said, "we want you to go back in and continue the hearing. Keep the attention of the audience focused on the front of the room. Ginger, come with us and identify the suspects."

Mr. Hixler reached the door just as the *Daily Journal* photographer burst through, followed by the school-district secretary.

"I told him not to come out here," the secretary said.

The photographer snapped pictures of the police, and of Ginger and Karie.

Mr. Hixler quickly stepped into the room, followed by the secretary. "Please dim the lights," he said as he clicked the Start button on the remote control. Mr. Wren's voice filled the room as the video played again.

Ginger and Karie hurried down the hall with the two police officers. They rounded the corner into the lobby and saw that the lobby was empty.

"He was standing in that doorway," Ginger said, pointing, "but he isn't there now."

Quietly, they slipped into the hearing room, where Ginger's video was still running. Ginger scanned the crowd.

"Do you see him?" Officer Tyle whispered.

"No," Ginger said.

"Which one is Joyce?"

Ginger pointed.

Outside, sirens wailed to a stop.

Officer Tyle motioned for the girls to go back to the lobby. "Can you describe him?" she asked Ginger.

Ginger told what the man looked like and what he was wearing. When she mentioned the Fred's Fish House logo on the baseball cap, Officer Tyle said, "Good job. Most people don't remember specific details." Then she radioed the description.

Ginger and Karie watched as Officer Hayworth tapped Joyce on the shoulder, whispered something to her, and then led her out of the hearing room.

Joyce looked confused.

As they came into the lobby, Joyce saw Ginger. The expression on her face went from confusion to shock to rage.

"You called the police?" she cried. "You want them to arrest your own mother?"

Chapter Fifteen

THE POLICE READ JOYCE her rights.

"Is it a crime to talk to my daughter?" she asked.

"It's against the law to harass someone," Officer Hayworth said, "or to stalk her. Or try to kidnap her."

"I've done nothing wrong," Joyce insisted as Officer Hayworth led her out to the squad car. "This is my baby. My baby."

Officer Tyle said, "We'll need you to come to the station, too, Ginger. Are your parents here? Or someone else who can drive you? If not, I'll get a squad car for you."

"My dad will be here any minute," Karie said. "He'll do it." Officer Tyle handed Ginger a card with the address of the police station and then hurried out to the waiting police car.

Other police officers entered the building and began to search the rest rooms. Ginger saw whirling blue lights outside and saw patrol cars at every corner of the parking lot.

"Dad had a last-minute crisis at work," Karie told Ginger. "That's why I was late; I had to ask my neighbor for a ride."

While they waited for Karie's dad, Ginger and Karie stood in the back of the room.

The first video ended.

"Lights up!" Mr. Hixler called.

"After viewing this video," Mr. Hixler said, "it is my opinion that the charges against Mr. Wren are not justified. He is a fine coach, and Roosevelt should be proud to have him."

"I agree completely," said one of the other board members. "I move that we dismiss the petition."

"I second the motion," said another board member.

"Is there further discussion?" Mr. Hixler asked.

"Yes!" shouted Mrs. Vaughn. She didn't even bother to speak into the microphone. "I demand that we hear the rest of the speakers."

"In the interest of fairness," Mr. Hixler said, "I call the next speaker, Allison Sumner."

Mrs. Sumner walked to the microphone. "I will use

my time to watch three minutes of another video," she said.

Mr. Hixler quickly started Ginger's second video. This time, he got the section Ginger had spliced in the night before. It showed Mrs. Vaughn, Mr. Fields, and some other parents screaming at Mr. Wren during the game. It showed them booing the players and shouting, "We want the starters!"

Gasps arose from the audience and the school board members. When the three minutes were up, Mrs. Sumner said, "We desperately need a coach who teaches our children to be good sports. Mr. Wren is such a coach." She sat down.

Mr. Hixler called the next speaker, Mr. Fields. He said, "I am shamed by the last video. I know that life skills are more important than basketball skills, and I apologize to Mr. Wren and ask the board to retain him."

"Way to go, Dad!" exclaimed Susan.

The next two speakers said only, "I pass on my time to speak, and ask the board to retain Mr. Wren."

Mr. Hixler said, "It seems clear that there is no need to continue this hearing. Is there further discussion from the board?"

"I call for the question," said the woman who had seconded the motion.

Mr. Hixler said, "All in favor of dismissing the petition to fire Mr. Wren, signify by saying aye."

There was a chorus of ayes.

"Those opposed?" said Mr. Hixler.

Silence.

Mr. Hixler said, "Let the record reflect that the school board has unanimously voted to keep Mr. Bill Wren as coach of the girls' basketball team." He banged his gavel on the table. "This hearing is dismissed."

Several students jumped to their feet, cheering wildly. Ginger was astonished to see Polly Vaughn in the center of the group.

Mrs. Wren burst into tears and hugged her husband.

Mrs. Vaughn stomped up the aisle toward Ginger, her face flushed with rage.

"Here comes a thunderstorm," said Karie. "Take cover."

"That was *not* a smart move," Mrs. Vaughn said to Ginger, "but it will be a costly one."

"Laura and Mom had nothing to do with it," Ginger said. "They don't even know about the videos."

"That's no excuse. You knew your testimony would ruin your sister's business, and your mother's, too. Your mother and Laura were warned. If they didn't tell you, that's their mistake."

The crowd surged into the lobby. Mrs. Vaughn left without talking to anyone else.

Ginger watched her go. Mom and Laura may never speak to me again, she thought.

Nancy Randolph and her father came over to Ginger. "That was a brave thing to do," Mr. Randolph told Ginger.

"Dad would have been the next speaker, if the hearing had continued," Nancy said. "You probably saved Dad's job."

"And cost my sister hers," Ginger said.

Mr. Bradley arrived.

"We need to go to the police station," Karie told him.

"For what?"

"We'll tell you in the car," Karie said.

On their way to the police station, Ginger and Karie told Mr. Bradley all that had happened. When she got to the part where the man said he had Tipper, Ginger's stomach knotted with anxiety. Had the police located Tipper? Was he okay?

"You should have told your parents," Mr. Bradley said.

"I was going to when they got home," Ginger said.

Mr. Bradley didn't say anything else, but Ginger knew he was right. She should have called Mom or Dad, or at least told a teacher what was going on. What if the man and Joyce had not agreed to wait while she spoke at the hearing? What if they had forced her to go with them?

The police station was an old flagstone building. Mr. Bradley and Karie went in with Ginger. An officer led them past an information desk, down a hall, and into a windowless room that contained a cluttered desk, four chairs, file cabinets, and a small table. A fax machine and a coffeepot shared the tabletop.

Soon Officer Hayworth came in. "Tipper is safe," he told Ginger. "He has been at his friend's house all along."

Relief poured over Ginger. Tipper drove her crazy sometimes with his jokes and his burping and his loud cowboy games, but if anything bad had happened to him, she would not have been able to stand it.

"We told your sister where you are," he added.

"Thank you."

"Laura's curiosity must be killing her," Karie said.

"Please tell me exactly what happened," the officer said.

Ginger started with her birthday lunch at the restaurant and told him everything. He asked some questions, and she answered them.

When she finished he said, "A fingerprint check on Joyce Enderly revealed an outstanding warrant for her arrest on a kidnapping charge. Three years ago, Enderly kidnapped a ten-year-old girl in Bozeman, Montana, and tried to convince the girl that Enderly was her mother."

Ginger felt sick to her stomach.

"The child escaped at a freeway rest stop," Officer Hayworth said, "and asked other travelers for help. One of them called police on a cellular phone, and Enderly drove off, leaving the girl behind. Her car was found abandoned in the next town. The police have been searching for Enderly ever since."

"If you had gone with Joyce and the man," Karie said, "they would have kidnapped you, too." She reached for Ginger's hand and held tight, as if she feared Ginger might still be snatched away.

"Since Joyce Enderly is a fugitive," Officer Hayworth said, "she's being held without bail."

"What about the man who was with her?"

"We're still looking for him."

Oh, great, Ginger thought. She wondered how much Joyce had told him. Did he know Ginger's name, and where she lived? What if he tried to get even with her for calling the police?

"You are free to go," Officer Hayworth said, "although we may want to talk to you again later."

"Do you and Laura want to stay at our house tonight?" Mr. Bradley asked as he drove Ginger home. "We can wait while you get your things."

"I'd love to," Ginger said, "but you don't need to wait. Laura has an early class on Saturdays, so she'll want the car at your house. We'll drive over."

"I'll make popcorn," Karie said. "I'm too excited to sleep."

When the car stopped in front of Ginger's house, Laura opened the door immediately. Once inside, Ginger related the whole story.

When she had finished, Laura hugged her and said, "What a terrible ordeal to go through. We should have—"

"I know," Ginger said. "We should have called Mom and Dad."

"It's partly my fault. When you told me that woman had called here and that she waited for you at school and wanted to talk to you, I should have called Mom or Dad. But I never dreamed she would do anything like this." Laura hugged Ginger again. "You're safe, and that's all that matters now."

"There's something else I need to tell you," Ginger said. She wondered if Laura would be so understanding when she learned that Ginger had alienated B.A. Catering's most important customer.

How do you tell your sister that you blew her chance to stay in college?

Chapter Sixteen

"I SPOKE AT THE HEARING," Ginger said. "I gave the school board some videotapes of Mr. Wren that proved he's a good coach, and the petition against him was dismissed. Mrs. Vaughn got really angry at me and she'll never hire you or Mom again."

Ginger kept her eyes on the floor, not wanting to see her sister's reaction. She talked faster and faster, needing to say everything and get it over with.

"I'm sorry, Laura. I didn't want to wreck your business, or Mom's, but nobody else had any proof and Mr. Wren was going to leave our school if he got fired, and his family would have to move, and he'd never get another coaching job, and it was so unfair that I—"

"You did the right thing."

"What?" Ginger looked up.

"You did the right thing," Laura repeated, "and I'm proud of you."

Ginger's eyes filled with tears. "You aren't mad at me?"

"Of course not. Mrs. Vaughn is a bully, and I'm glad you had the guts to stand up and tell the truth."

"But your catering business! She'll tell all her friends not to hire you, and you won't have enough money for your tuition."

"I'm tired of cutting up broccoli and making tiny little cream puffs," Laura said. "I think I'll apply for a part-time job as a cook in one of the dorms, where I could prepare *real* food, like waffles and big baked potatoes. I can probably earn even more than I have with B.A. Catering."

"I wrecked Mom's business, too. She's going to hate me when she finds out."

"I doubt that."

Just then the phone rang. Ginger jumped as if a rifle had gone off in the room. She hadn't realized her nerves were so taut.

"This is Officer Tyle. I thought you'd like to know we have the man in custody. A police dog tracked him to some shrubbery in the green belt behind the administration building."

Ginger felt the tension float out of her. She thanked Officer Tyle for calling and relayed the news to Laura.

"You need to call Mom and Dad," Laura said.

"I'd rather not tell them about Joyce over the phone," Ginger said. "Do you think I can wait until they get home?"

"No," Laura said. "You have to call tonight."

"Now that Joyce and the man are both in custody, the danger is over."

"What about the newspaper photographer who was there? And the TV reporters who listen to the police scanners? The story will be on tonight's news. It could get picked up by one of the networks and broadcast in Chicago or Atlanta."

Ginger found the note her mother had left, with the hotel phone number on it. When she finished telling her mother what had happened, Mrs. Shaw said, "I'll be home as soon as I can get a flight."

"But the wedding is tomorrow! I'm perfectly safe now; there's no need for you to come home early."

"I'm going to call the police, and your father," Mrs. Shaw said, "and then I'll decide what to do. I'll call you back."

Ginger gave her Officer Tyle's name, and the phone number off the business card. Half an hour later, Mrs. Shaw called. "The police assured me that there's no need to worry," she said, "so I'm going to stay for the wedding and come home as planned. Mrs. Thomas is on her way over; she'll stay with you and Laura until Sunday."

Ginger didn't protest.

Mrs. Shaw ended the conversation in her usual way: "I love you."

"Love you, too."

Ginger called Karie to tell her the man had been caught. "We'll stay here tonight," Ginger said. "Tell your dad thanks for the invitation, but Mom has Mrs. Thomas coming to stay with us."

"Good idea," Karie said.

For the first time in a week, Ginger slept soundly. When she woke up Saturday morning, splinters of sunshine patterned the floor near the window. She did not look to see if the white car was parked outside. She fed Flopsy, then went to the kitchen. She poured a glass of juice and sat down beside Mrs. Thomas, who was reading the morning newspaper.

"It says here," Mrs. Thomas told Ginger, "that the woman who claimed to be your mother has a long history of mental illness." She handed the paper to Ginger.

Three stories shared the front page. A picture of the man in the Fred's Fish House cap, being led away in handcuffs by the police, accompanied the first story.

SUSPECTS NABBED AT SCHOOL HEARING

Two people were arrested last night at the Roosevelt School District Administration Building for the attempted abduction of Ginger Shaw, a thirteen-year-old student. They were identified as Joyce Enderly and Jake Gallo, both of Seattle.

Enderly, whose legal name is Joyce Gallo, is wanted by the police for the abduction three years ago of a ten-year-old Montana girl. The girl escaped at a freeway rest stop, and other travelers called 911 on a cellular phone. Joyce Enderly's husband, Arnold Gallo, was sentenced to prison for the crime. Enderly eluded capture.

Ginger wondered if the child's escape, and the imprisonment of Joyce's husband, were the "small problem" she had referred to.

Seven years before that incident, Enderly was sentenced to a psychiatric hospital after snatching a three-year-old girl from a store in Seattle. She was discharged after eight months but was in other psychiatric hospitals prior to the Montana abduction. Psychiatrists who have treated Enderly testified in court that she did not believe that her own child had died at birth and she suffers from delusions that these other children are hers.

Ginger shuddered at her close call, and kept reading:

Enderly began trailing Shaw last Saturday. When Shaw refused to meet with her alone, Enderly hired her brother-in-law, Jake Gallo, to help arrange a meeting with Shaw. The pair was arrested after Shaw signaled a friend, Karie Bradley, for help. Bradley called police.

Ginger went on to the second article, which featured a photo of Ginger handing her tapes to Mr. Hixler. Ginger wished she hadn't cut her hair so short.

A second picture showed Mr. Wren surrounded by happy students. The headline said "Roosevelt Coach Retained." Smiling, Ginger read the article.

The third front-page article said:

LOCAL SOCIALITE ACCUSED OF COERCION

Victoria Vaughn, wife of Vaughn Enterprises CEO Claude Vaughn, was accused last night of threatening to withhold business from local people who supported Mr. Bill Wren in the Roosevelt School District controversy. Mrs. Vaughn had filed the petition to remove Wren as coach of the girls' basketball team.

Before yesterday's hearing, Kevin Bradley, an executive with Elite Advertising, called the Daily Journal with a list of people who, he said, had been contacted by Mrs. Vaughn.

Ginger wondered if Karie knew her dad had called the newspaper. She continued reading:

When the Journal questioned those people, all of them said that Victoria Vaughn had pressured them to speak against Wren and had implied that if they did not do so, they would lose future business with Vaughn Enterprises. Those people are:

Mr. Randolph was the first name on the list. Ginger skimmed down the rest of the names, astonished to see that Laura was one of them. No wonder she wasn't angry with me, Ginger thought. She had already taken a public stand herself.

The article concluded:

Victoria Vaughn was not available for comment. However, a spokesperson for Vaughn Enterprises stated that the company does not sanction such tactics and that no business will be withheld because of testimony in the Wren case.

"I wonder if Mrs. Vaughn will ever ask Mom to plan a party again," Ginger said.

"I predict she will," Mrs. Thomas said. "She has been thoroughly embarrassed by this article; she'll want to pretend that she did nothing wrong."

Ginger had just finished reading the front page when Tipper and Marcus rushed in. They each carried a can of root beer, and Tipper waved a copy of the

Daily Journal. "You got your name in the paper!" he shouted.

"Twice!" yelled Marcus.

"And your picture!" Tipper said.

"I know."

"It says that woman *was* spying on you!" Tipper was so excited, his voice squeaked. "Why didn't you tell me? Marcus and I could have helped you. We could have trapped her and tied her to a tree!"

Ginger smiled at her brother. "I know you could have," she said, "but I didn't want to put you in danger."

"Next time, tell us," Tipper said. "We'll protect you. If that woman in the white car comes around again, we'll spray shaving cream on the windows so she can't see to drive away. We'll put tacks in the street and give her a flat tire. We'll . . ." Tipper paused for breath.

"Next time, I'll ask for your help," Ginger said, although she knew that with Joyce in custody there would not be a next time.

"Are you boys drinking root beer for breakfast?" Mrs. Thomas asked, her tone implying that they were ruining their health forever.

"It isn't our breakfast," Tipper said. "It's our teaching tool."

"Sweetie, your teeth will rot and fall out if you drink pop all day long," Mrs. Thomas said.

"They didn't print all the news," Tipper grumbled. "We looked through the whole paper, and they left out a really important story."

"Oh?" said Ginger. "What's that?"

"The notice about our burping school. We named ourselves The Big Bold Burpers, and we wrote a story about our lessons, and Marcus's mom drove us to the *Daily Journal* office so we could turn it in."

"Maybe they'll print your notice tomorrow," Ginger said. "There was a lot of local news today."

"We spent all our money on twelve cans of root beer, and now we need more pupils," Tipper said. "Do you want to come? We'll give you lessons for half price."

"No, thanks. I already know how to burp."

"Not as good as we do," said Tipper.

Both boys took huge gulps of root beer and loudly demonstrated their skill.

Peg Kehret lives in a log house in the woods near Mount Rainier National Park in Washington State. She and her husband, Carl, have two grown children and four grandchildren.

Peg's popular books often appear on recommended lists from the International Reading Association and the American Library Association. They are regularly nominated for young readers' awards, which she has won many times. *I'm Not Who You Think I Am* is her thirtieth book.

An animal lover and Humane Society volunteer, Peg also likes to read, pump her player piano, and watch baseball.